The Pinfire Lady

P.J. Gallagher

A Black Horse Western

ROBERT HALE

© P.J. Gallagher 2019
First published in Great Britain 2019

ISBN 978-0-7198-2956-7

The Crowood Press
The Stable Block
Crowood Lane
Ramsbury
Marlborough
Wiltshire SN8 2HR

www.bhwesterns.com

Robert Hale is an imprint
of The Crowood Press

Dedicated to my wife Maureen, aka Mo M. Down

Typeset by
Derek Doyle & Associates, Shaw Heath
Printed and bound in Great Britain by
4Bind Ltd, Stevenage, SG1 2XT

CHAPTER ONE

'Damn him!' Abigail, Lady Penraven, slipped from the saddle and threw herself down on the short, coarse grass of the little clearing. Pounding her fist on the ground, she uttered a string of most unladylike expletives, overheard over the years from men of her father's regiment. At the same time, a whole series of different emotions rushed through her mind. Of these, uppermost was anger; coupled with sadness at her betrayal; humiliation at the situation in which she found herself, and a sense of inadequacy.

Abigail had left the wagon train intending to go for but a short ride, to exercise the big bay gelding she had bought before leaving Independence. Something had prompted her to return. Some inner sense had warned her all was not well. She had quietly ridden back to the encircled wagons and, dismounting, had walked over to the steps secured at the back of their wagon, ignoring the half-embarrassed, half-pitying looks she received from their neighbours. Even before mounting the steps, she heard female giggles, and a male muttering from within.

Quickly, she stepped up and peered inside. Her worst suspicions were realized when she observed Bertram Penraven, her husband, and Yvette, her French-Canadian maid, engaged in passionate love making.

Yvette had uttered a little scream and Bertie, interrupted in his sexual endeavours, had looked back over his shoulder to see the outraged figure of his wife, Abigail, staring at the two half-clothed figures before her,

'O Lor', Abbie!' he cried as she turned away in disgust. 'I can explain. . . !'

Abbie did not stay to listen to the remainder of his lies. Aboard her bay, she tore out of the encampment and, with the horse at full gallop, had thundered across the undulating vista of prairie, heedless of her direction. There was a red mist before her eyes, while the pounding hoofs seemed to be mocking her constant thought. 'He promised! He promised! He promised!'

Eventually, she had slowed the sweat-lathered gelding to a walk and looked about her. She had entered an area where there was a rocky outcrop, evidence of some cataclysmic upheaval in eons past. Abbie's route led her into a small, cleared area about the size of a tennis court, nearly surrounded by boulders and rocks of grey granite. And there, in this solitude, she had given vent to all the pent up feelings that had been part of her nearly three years of marriage to Lord Bertram Penraven – the petty humiliations, the broken promises of a drunken sot, who preferred the attentions of barmaids and the like, rather than seek the woman who had occupied his marriage bed.

Finally, her blind rage began to subside and she became more conscious of her surroundings while, at the same time, a swirling kaleidoscope of memories welled up one after another. There were the years in India, tenderly cared for by Marta her Ayah, who had taken the place of her own mother who, worn out by the constant humid heat and frequently bed-ridden, had finally succumbed to a tropical fever. Major Frederick Martin, her father, had continued to offer the bluff love that he had always shown his little daughter, but inevitably his military responsibilities took precedence and therefore the raising of little Abbie had been left to the Indian girl, Marta.

As time had passed, Abbie had taken more notice of the world around her; the cantonment, with its small married quarters, bungalows; the garrison church where she was taken every Sunday in her best white dress, and forced to sit, without too much wriggling, to long grown-up sermons delivered by the Reverend Mr Williams, the regimental Chaplain. Then there was the regiment itself, the Royal Berkshire Light Infantry and, more especially, D Company, which her father commanded. In her early days, she had clutched Marta's hand tightly as she watched, one thumb stuck firmly in her mouth, while the company was drilled on the square by Company Sergeant Major Jones, he with the loud terrifying voice, who in later years, she found, was like putty in her hands, as she wheedled some small favour from him.

The years had passed and, as she grew older, her father took to taking her with him when he went on safaris up into the Kashmiri hill country. During these treks, Abbie learned the rudiments of finding comfort in but a primitive camp, and more importantly, developed into a reasonable shot with both a .24 gauge shotgun, and also a

7

small .25 calibre rook rifle. As she had grown in size and strength, so her skills with firearms of still larger calibre improved, till the day arrived when she triumphantly bagged an Indian deer, using the then standard British military rifle, the 1853 pattern, percussion .577 calibre, Enfield.

Sadly it was but a short time after that that Major Martin had received a mortal wound from a round fired by a jezail-wielding Afridi, and seventeen-year-old Abbie had found herself an orphan. Despite her tearful pleas to remain in India, Major Martin's will had been quite clear. In the event of his demise, Abbie was to be sent to England to live with his brother George's family. Apparently this had all been arranged between the two brothers, when the Major's wife first exhibited signs of the debilitation that was to slowly, but inexorably, drag her to a lonely grave far from the land for which she had constantly, but secretly, yearned.

Abbie Martin did not like England, with its cold damp climate for so much of the year. Nor did she manage to establish a warm relationship with Aunt Sarah, Uncle George's wife, a shrewish woman of icy temperament, who was always picking holes in Abbie's deportment and mode of speech, and deploring the education that had been imparted by the Reverend Mr. Williams.

'Don't do this, Abigail! Don't do that, Abigail. Well brought up young ladies do not enter conversations which deal with topics that are purely a male domain!' This last admonition was her reaction when Abbie had startled an assembled company by daring to describe the impact effect of a rifled bullet upon an Indian deer. She was stifled and depressed by her inability to resign herself to an endless future of soirees, dainty tea cups and mindless gossip about clothing, fashions and the wayward exploits of those not present.

It was no wonder that the lonely, friendless girl was easily swept off her feet by the attentions of a youthful neighbour, Lord Bertram Penraven. There was a whirl-wind courtship, followed by a society wedding about which Aunt Sarah was, for once, wildly enthusiastic. Harsh reality emerged, shortly after the wedding, as Abbie Penraven rapidly became aware of the truth of her situation. Her debonair spouse was a wastrel drunkard, who pursued any-thing in the female form – except his own wife, whom he had apparently married only for her dowry and to gain access to certain investments which, Abbie learned, had been made in her name when she was but a child. These investments would appear to be the product of extensive travelling her father had undertaken many years before her birth. Apparently while still single, the then Lieutenant Martin had taken an extended furlough and had spent some considerable time in the western United States. In fact he was one of the early prospectors who found pay dirt in what was to become a gold rush to equal that which was shortly to take place in California.

Hounded by his creditors, and promising to reform, Bertram had proposed that they travel to the United States and examine the situation regarding the major's invest-ments, about which there was apparently a mystery. The investments included major shares in a mining operation in Colorado, one of the western Territories though, at that time, still part of Kansas. After an initial dividend, there had been no further word regarding the success of the mining operation. Agreement was reached regarding the need to clear up the American mystery, and Abbie thought that being away from his regular haunts might aid Bertram in his professed attempts to reform.

The Atlantic voyage had been uneventful, as had the coach journey on the Cumberland road as far west as the Mississippi. Crossing the great river, they continued west as far as Independence, where wagon trains assembled before journeying across the Great American Desert, otherwise known as the prairie. At Independence, the English couple had purchased a sturdy wagon known as a 'Prairie Schooner', and a full team of oxen to draw their conveyance. A rather uncouth teamster, Caleb Otter, whose habit of continually spitting tobacco juice Abbie found more than a little disturbing, had been hired to handle the team and, at the last minute, Bertram had suggested that Abbie should have the services of a personal maid. Reluctantly, Abbie had agreed, and Yvette, the attractive, vivacious little French-Canadian was added to their party.

Was it a pre-conceived plan on Bertram's part to add another female, and had he already encountered Yvette during his many strolls around the little frontier settlement? Abbie never knew but, from that time on, there had been a subtle change in the relationship of the quartet travelling westward.

A distant sound of gunshots, accompanied by wild screams and whoops, broke in upon the distraught girl's recollections. Startled she rose from the grass and, drawing her father's small brass telescope from its leather case, she clambered up some of the rocks enclosing the clearing and focused the instrument in the direction of the encampment. The lenses brought the full horror of the Indian attack much closer to her, and she crouched down terrified lest keen eyes observed her up in her eyrie. She need not have worried about disclosure.

The mounted attack had moved from its initial operation of riding around the wagons, pouring in clouds of arrows and the occasional musket shot. Now, upon a signal from a war-bonneted figure directing the attack from some distance away, raising high a lance, the circling riders turned and drove their horses at the gaps between each wagon. Although some fell to the defenders' frantic fire, the majority were successful in breaching the defence and, from her elevated position, Abbie could see desperate figures attempting to avoid their ghastly fate.

One figure leapt over a wagon tongue and, mad with fear, fled into the open prairie, pursued by a tomahawk-flourishing Indian warrior. Focusing on the trouserless white man, she could see it was her faithless husband Bertram, screaming with fear, as the pounding hoofs of his horse-borne nemesis drew ever closer. Seconds later, the horse was alongside, and the tomahawk rose and fell, buried between Bertram's shoulder blades. The Indian let out a triumphant yell, and Abbie sank down upon the rocks, oblivious to the fact that she was suddenly now a widow. She was horrified, yet still compelled to watch the remainder of the distant tragedy which, like some ghastly play, was taking place before her eyes brought sharply into focus by Major Martin's field telescope.

Her late husband's killer leapt from his dappled pony and, jumping astride Bertram's corpse, proceeded to pass

11

a knife around his victim's head with an efficiency born of much practice. In no time, he was waving aloft his Lordship's blond and now bloody hair.

The last of the defenders had now been killed and scalped, and the scene resembled something from Dante's *Inferno*. Naked and near-naked braves were dancing war dances and waving aloft bloody bunches of hair, while others looted the wagons that were already burning from the arrows launched during the initial attack. The wagons' contents were being dragged out and scattered on the bloody grass, not with any systematic order, but appearing more like the wilful reaction of a large number of bad-tempered children.

Abbie had reopened her eyes once more, in time to see, feel and hear the effect of a massive explosion, as one government wagon, containing a large number of gunpowder barrels, caught fire and exploded, sending pieces of the wagon, together with parts of Indian bodies, high into the air.

Almost at the same time there was a series of lightning flashes, followed immediately by crashes of thunder, as a violent storm burst upon the scene. The coincidence of explosion and storm may well have convinced the Indians that Manitou was angry with them, for suddenly they dropped much of the looted material and, springing upon their ponies, fled.

Abbie meanwhile had slid down the rocks and, soaked to the skin, had crouched against a slight overhang in the vain hope of seeking some relief from the relentless downpour. Luckily she'd remembered to leave the bay's reins hanging down in front of him. He had hardly moved from where she had dismounted and, temporarily leaving her illusion of shelter, she ran to where the bay patiently waited, and dragged him over to stand with her against the rocky wall. So passed the most miserable night of Abbie's existence. Buffeted by continuous gusts of rain-laden wind, and half deafened by the noise of the thunder, horse and girl waited out the night.

CHAPTER TWO

Gradually the storm drove on towards the east, where a faint light along the horizon heralded the coming dawn. During the terròrs of the night Abbie had been doing some hard thinking, and it was now that the skills learned with her father on their treks together stood her in good stead. First, she had to get off some of her wet clothing, hanging in soaking clammy folds around her. She stripped to the bare skin, her lithe young body shivering in the cool, damp, morning air and her nipples hardening involuntarily. Then she wrung out her cotton blouse, chemise and pantalettes and donned them, with the thought that, being of light cotton, they would dry fairly quickly. Her heavy riding habit of jacket and ankle-length skirt she bundled up and tied behind her saddle.

Now she had to forage the abandoned camp looking for specific things – food, utensils, a blanket and, most important, weapons with which to defend herself against both wild animals and wild men.

Mounting the bay from a convenient boulder, Abbie settled herself with a little grimace in the wet side-saddle and rode cautiously across the sodden prairie towards the devastated wagon train. Nearing the site she paused momentarily, looking down on the thing that had once been her husband. Curiously she felt no particular emotion, not even disgust or horror, at the partially disrobed corpse, with its hairless, reddened skull; he was no longer part of her existence.

She entered the enclosure formed by the burnt, partially burnt and destroyed wagons, appalled by not merely the human death all around her, but also the wanton slaughter of the oxen. There Caleb Otter slumped, pinned to a wagon by an Indian lance, still with a brown stream of tobacco juice drooling down his dead whiskery face. Close by lay Yvette, on her back, her golden hair gone, now no doubt adorning some Indian's lance or tippee. Her throat had been cut from ear to ear and, in a final parody of her illicit sexual adventures, a broken lance was thrust up between her bare legs.

Shuddering, Abbie dismounted and, tying the bay to a wagon wheel, she set about obtaining some of the things she desperately needed. Quickly, she gathered up a blanket, burnt along one edge but still serviceable, a small skillet and several scattered cans which, hopefully, contained food. The Penraven wagon was still standing, relatively untouched, apart from a ripped and burnt tilt. There was a secret compartment behind the driver's seat, and Abbie prayed that it had not been discovered. Climbing up into the front of the wagon, she reached down and slid the panel aside. The first thing her searching fingers discovered was a small bundle of papers, which she drew out and put to one side. They could wait.

The remaining object she eagerly seized upon was a case about eighteen inches long, by nine or ten inches wide, and about four inches deep. Trembling slightly, Abbie unfastened the case and drew out its principal content. In her hands was a long-barrelled pistol; her mind swept back to her Uncle George's study, and their final meeting before she and Bertram had left for Liverpool and the ship that would take them to the New World.

'Abbie, I want you to accept this little gift from me. You'll probably never have to use it, but you're going to a strange wild land and anything could happen.'

Opening the box, he had shown and demonstrated the contents. He pointed out that the pistol had the name 'Tipping and Lawden – London' engraved on the barrel and stressed that it had been proofed, that is, tested thoroughly by the London Proof House who had verified that the gun was safe to use. He explained patiently that, despite its markings, the pistol was not of English origin.

'This is a 12mm pinfire revolver, designed by a rather clever French chap, name of Lefaucheux. Unlike the pistols now being produced at the Colt factory on the south bank in London, these are not loaded from the front of the cylinder with powder and ball. Here.' He had paused, and extracted a small brass tube, which had a dull lead appearance at one end and a small pin projecting from the side. 'This is called a cartridge. When this gate is raised on the right side of the pistol, the cartridge is slipped into the empty chamber, and the pin projects through this little slot here.

'If the gun is cocked, and the trigger squeezed, the

hammer will fall onto the pin and the pistol will fire. Since the cylinder has six chambers, one can fire six shots without reloading. It is a fairly simple matter to push out the used cartridges with this rod, mounted on the side, and then reload.'

Uncle George had then patiently explained the remainder of the case's contents: a small screwdriver for disassembling the pistol, a compartment containing a large quantity of the novel 'pinfire' cartridges, and a small steel tube.

'This is called a "chimney piece". In the unlikely event that you have no more cartridges, this can be loaded as one would a muzzle loading weapon, inserted into a chamber, and a cap placed upon the projecting chimney where the pin would normally be. Thus, one would still have a single shot with which to defend oneself. Abbie, I know that your father instructed you in the use of firearms. Promise me you will keep this weapon handy.'

Abbie had so promised, and, despite Bertram's protestations that he was quite capable of protecting his wife, or for that matter any woman, she had kept the pistol with her belongings when they left for America.

Returning to the present, Abbie loaded the pinfire pistol and, rummaging around, found a long red scarf which she fashioned into a sash around her waist. Thus attired, she thrust her pistol into the sash, the way she had seen Sowers of the Indian cavalry carry their pistols, and gathering her other 'finds' together, including a man's slouch hat, she left the wagon and, noting regretfully that the Indians had not left behind a single long gun, mounted her horse and

17

rode off across the prairie.

She headed in a roughly south-western direction. There were two reasons for her choice. The Indian war party had come from the north and returned in that direction and she had no desire to encounter that body of bloodthirsty devils. Secondly, several days prior, the wagon train had been diverted from the regular trail to the north-west, by visible signs of a huge prairie fire southward, and it had been hoped that, by swinging north, they would escape the conflagration. The move had been successful, but ultimately had dire results.

Abbie theorized that eventually she should be able to recognize the well-worn tracks of the Sante Fe Trail and, possibly meet up with another group of wagons heading west, or eventually reach some western settlement where she could obtain both supplies and assistance.

Her immediate concern was to find water for herself and the bay. The last halt of the wagon train had been a dry camp and, entering the area after the storm, she had noted that the barrels lashed to the sides of the wagons had all suffered in the fighting or the subsequent explosion. Thus, although she had found a canteen still containing a trickle of hopefully pure water, it was absolutely essential that, if she and her horse were to survive, they should locate a source of the life-giving fluid.

So Abbie rode on, slouched in the uncomfortable side saddle, her head constantly turning as her eyes swept the horizon on the lookout for signs of hostile natives, and evidence of either civilization or water. The sun beat down from a brilliant blue sky and, although lacking the humidity she had experienced years earlier in India, she found that she was gradually becoming more and more thirsty and drowsy, despite taking occasional sips from her canteen. The bay too was starting to experience difficulties and once he stumbled, sending Abbie's heart pounding.

Peering from under the battered old hat acquired during her scavenging, Abbie noted a dark line running across the prairie, and a while later it revealed itself as the tops of a line of trees. Trees indicated the presence of water and she urged on the weary animal. 'Come on, boy! We'll soon have water!'

The cottonwoods lined both banks of a small creek that ran diagonally across her route and, thankfully, Abbie dismounted and led the horse down the bank to where a stream of water four or five feet wide trickled merrily on its way. Both horse and girl lowered their heads and lapped up the crystal clear water, feeling greatly refreshed as they replaced their lost fluids.

Abbie stood and looked around. Suddenly, she sensed that she and the bay were not alone. Crouching, she pulled out the pinfire pistol and cocked the hammer, sweeping the gun back and forth, as she attempted to determine the source of her unease.

'S'all right, boy! I ain't gonna hurt you. Even iffen I could, which I can't.'

Abbie peered closer, and found a figure propped against the trunk of a tree. Dragging the unwilling horse behind her and with her pistol firmly grasped in her right hand and steadied against her body, Abbie approached the voice.

She found that she was looking down at a grey-

19

bearded, bald-headed man clad in greasy buckskins. One arm hung awkwardly from his shoulder, where his coat was ripped and bloody, and one leg, obviously broken, was buckled under him. Nearby was the body of a large bear, beneath whose carcase could be seen the stock of a long gun.

'Howdy, boy! As you can see, ol' Griz here has left me in a bit of a fix.'

Suddenly, his eyes opened wide as, looking more closely at the lightly-dressed figure before him, he realized that he was making a terrible blunder in identification.

'Well, Jiminy! I can certainly see you ain't no boy, ma'am. Beggin' your pardon, but I sure didn't 'spect to see no she-males in this neck o' the woods! Who are you, an' whatcha doing here in that getup?'

Abbie, ignoring her title, introduced herself as Abbie Penraven, and gave a brief outline of what had happened to the wagon train, ignoring her husband's role in the massacre with the sudden realization that, if his infidelity had not happened, she would not have ridden off and therefore would have also been one of the victims of the attack.

'Well, Abbie, I am sure glad to meet you, though not like this, ma'am. Name's Billy Curtis. Came out west with ma folks when I was jus' a wee'n. Family came from Tennessee, but they're all gone now.'

Billy went on to describe how he had been tracking the grizzly that lay dead before them, and the crafty animal, typical of the species, had circled round behind him and suddenly attacked. He had managed to get off one shot with his Hawken plains rifle, before the bear was upon

20

him, and after that it was a fight with his Bowie knife against the bear's teeth and ripping claws. He had managed to get in a mortal blow with his blade but, in stepping back, had stumbled over a fallen bough and fell awkwardly, thus breaking his left leg. And there he had lain, unable to move to any degree, hoping that the periodic shivers and twitches that went through the grizzly were merely part of its death throes, and not an indication that it was reviving to continue the contest.

'Ma'am, iffen you could git ma Bowie from that thar bear, I figure we could rig somethin' up. That is, if you've a mind to help me.'

Abbie was a trifle indignant. 'Mr Curtis, of course I'll assist you in any way I can! Do you really think that I would even consider going off and leaving a fellow human being in such dire circumstances?'

Suitably abashed, Billy apologised, muttering that he wasn't used to dealing with ladies. At least not of Abbie's type, thinking of some of the sporting girls he had known in times past, when the fires of life had burned more brightly.

'Well now, to business!' He went on to state that their first task must be to retrieve his Bowie knife and, that accomplished, suitable branches could be cut to furnish splints for his leg, and then make what he called a travois. He had noted that Abbie's saddle had a lariat hanging from the right side. Abbie, when first obtaining the bay weeks ago, had queried the addition of the plaited rawhide line, suggesting that she had no intention of herding cattle, but had been cautioned to leave it be, as it might be useful some day. And now it was.

21

Under Billy Curtis' directions, Abbie tied one end of the lariat securely around one of the forelegs of the grizzly, put the line in a clove hitch around the pommel of her saddle, and then back around the hind leg of the animal. Leading the bay by his headstall, she coaxed him to move slowly away as the lines tightened. As the lariat took up the tension, so gradually the grizzly was rolled onto his back, exposing the knife buried up to the haft in his chest. Billy called out to Abbie to halt the horse, which she did and, hurrying back, with considerable effort withdrew the knife from the body.

With the Bowie, Abbie chopped down two slender saplings with which to create splints, and longer pieces from which to make the travois.

'Now little lady, you are gonna hurt me, but it has to be done.' Abbie bit her lower lip but nodded in agreement. 'We gotta straighten that leg an' then pull it out so that the broken pieces fit together, otherwise t'will heal crookedly.'

Trembling slightly, Abbie did as she was told, pulling Billy's left leg out straight, while the latter grimaced with pain. Then when Billy was ready, she hauled on his moccasin-covered foot, allowing the broken bones to fit together. The splints were laid either side of the injured leg and bound in place with pieces of lariat, then working together, the travois was constructed, with Abbie cutting and fetching the required pieces of wood, while Billy, using more pieces of lariat, lashed the cross pieces to the two long poles.

The travois poles were secured either side of the saddle and Billy rolled himself onto their rude conveyance. With

Abbie walking and leading her horse and Billy Curtis sitting on the travois with his loaded rifle across his lap, the strange party set off westward.

CHAPTER THREE

During the making of the travois, the ill-assorted couple had discussed their projected route, and had agreed to a compromise. Abbie had explained to Billy something of her need to reach the mining camps and how, when she and her late husband had first joined the wagon train, it was understood that the intended route would be the Santa Fe Trail, past Council Grove and Pawnee Rock, and then about seventy-five miles further on, where the trail divided, the Wagon Master intended to take the right fork known as the Mountain Division which led into Colorado Territory. All she knew now was that she was somewhere north of the trail close to Pawnee Rock.

The old trapper thought that her surmise was pretty good, for what he privately considered was a mere she-male, but stressed that there were other factors to be taken into consideration. A supply of food was essential. While the weather remained fine it was all right, but it was now late Fall, and if snow started they would need clothing, food and shelter. As a last resort, they could head for a cabin that he had tucked away in the foot hills. And that was how things had stood between them when they started off.

At first the bay objected to being turned into a draft animal, but he soon settled down and plodded along while Abbie had a firm grip upon his halter. There was little in the way of conversation. Billy, riding uncomfortably on the travois, kept his eyes on the horizon behind them and voiced his concern at the travois marks leaving a trail which a child could follow.

Abigail too was busy, watching the area ahead of them, guiding the bay and silently grimacing at her fashionable riding boots, which had never been designed for tramping across the prairie.

With the sun high overhead, Billy called a halt to their march to which Abbie thankfully agreed. Her arm ached from holding the bay's halter and her feet felt as though they were on fire. Exhausted, she sank down by the travois and took small sips, as instructed, from the water bottle.

Billy handed her what looked like a dried up and blackened twig. 'Here, chew on this, girlie. It'll give you some energy.'

Abbie accepted the offering dubiously.

'It's jerky!' he continued. 'Dried venison, cut into strips and dried in the sun. T'aint fancy but it'll keep you goin'.' Looking at Abbie's obvious discomfort caused by her elegant riding boots, he demanded. 'Git them boots off or they gonna cripple you.'

He rummaged around in what he called his possibles bag and produced several objects. The first was a small leather bag containing a quantity of tallow. Working this with his hand, he then massaged both of Abigail's feet with it to relieve the tenderness and the blisters that were rapidly forming.

Then he produced a pair of embroidered moccasins. 'Here put these on. Reckon they'll fit you mighty fine. Made them meself for a little Cheyenne gal I was partial to, but she went off with a handsome buck who'd taken a fancy to her. Meant to throw 'em away, jus' never got round to it.'

Billy's voice had become gruff as he made the offering of the footwear and Abbie realized that beneath the old trapper's coarse appearance there was a man with a sensitive caring nature. Gratefully she donned the moccasins, initially surprised at the soft comfort experienced by her sore and aching feet.

After a rest of about an hour they resumed their journey westward until the sun began to sink towards the horizon, when Billy called a halt at a shallow gully that would permit them to remain below the skyline. Under his directions Abbie built a very small fire using only dry twigs so that very little smoke was produced. Coffee was made and drank and then the fire was extinguished.

Abbie was surprised at Billy's next instruction. 'All right, girlie! Now we move on for a mile or so and find a secure place to bed down for the night. Fool anyone who might be creeping up on you.'

They moved on and found a place where a jutting rock could secure them from the rear of their little camp and there they settled for the night, taking turns to keep watch for intruders or hostile wild life.

The next four days passed in a similar fashion, but the fifth day was decidedly different. Halfway through the morning

Billy called upon Abigail to halt. 'There's riders coming up from behind us. Don't look as though they're Indians but even so, I ain't takin' any chances. There's some purty strange white folks around these parts.'

Abbie loosened her pistol still nestled in her sash. She had been tempted to put it in a saddle bag and be relieved of the weight. Now she was glad that some sixth sense had prompted her to keep it close at hand, hidden under her riding jacket which was thrown across her shoulders to help her ward off the fierce glare of the sun.

As the strangers drew near, Billy warned his partner. In a low voice he said, 'I know these scums. They ain't up to any good.' And in a louder tone, exclaimed. 'Well howdy, Jake! See you've still got your two side-kicks. Howdy, boys!'

The unprepossessing trio reined up close to the rear of the travois. All three were unwashed, with scruffy unshaven appearances. Their weapons, however, seemed to be serviceable and ready for use.

Jake the leader answered Billy's greeting with false heartiness. 'Well if it ain't my old pal Billy Curtis. Looks as though you've got yourself in a bit of a fix.' His wolfish grin as he spoke belied the would-be friendliness that he injected into his voice.

'And who have we got here?' he queried, turning his attention to Abbie who stood quietly, one hand under her jacket holding her pistol. 'Well, it looks as though Billy's got himself a little prairie chicken. T'aint fair, Billy! Surely you are gonna share with your friends.' So saying, he dismounted with the obvious intention of moving towards Abbie.

'Keep away from her, Jake! I'm warnin' ya.' The old

27

trapper struggled to position himself on the travois where he could bring his long gun to cover Jake, who merely laughed as he turned towards Abbie standing by the bay. His intent was obvious as he moved slowly towards her, licking his lips and staring at her with lascivious burning eyes.

Abbie cried out, 'Keep away from me!' So saying, she pulled out the pinfire pistol, holding it with both hands and cocking it with her left thumb as she aimed at the centre of Jake's leather fringed jacket.

Jake laughed and was still laughing as Abbie squeezed the trigger. The pistol roared in her hand and her target slumped down with both hands clutching his chest. 'God damn it, girl! You've done for me.'

Abbie ignored him as she swept her pistol to cover the other two. One, a Mexican, going by his wide sombrero, chose to ignore the pistol's message and went for a gun in a saddle boot. Abbie did not hesitate. Again she fired and the Mexican fell from the saddle with a hole in the bridge of his nose. The third man raised his hands and declared, 'I'm a-going, lady!'

And still with his hands held high, he manoeuvred his horse with his knees and rode off towards the east. Grey black smoke hung in the still air and the only noise was the sound of the receding hoof beats as the lone bandit vanished eastwards.

'Haw, haw, haw. Well, girlie, you sure gave ol' Jake the surprise of his life. Lemme see what kind of hawgleg did the trick.' As Billy said this, he held out his right hand for Abbie's pistol.

Without a thought, Abbie handed it over. In a flash Billy

had rolled the gun by its trigger guard and the girl found herself looking down the barrel of her own pistol. Frozen with fear, she stared open-mouthed at Billy's grim features and at the cocked pinfire aimed up at her head. Then Billy's visage relaxed into a smile and, lowering the hammer gently, he reversed the pistol and handed it back to his greatly relieved companion.

'Lesson *numero uno*, girlie! Never hand over any of yer guns 'less they're empty or 'less you've a second one covering the fella asking for a look-see. Watch iffen he tries to do the Border Roll as I did.'

'But Billy! You are my friend! Surely you don't expect a person to go through life without trusting anyone?'

Billy chuckled. 'Probably back East or over in Limeyland folks tend to be more trustin'. But this is the West an' you've got to look out for yourself! Now, enough of that subject, let's check ole Jake and his late buddy over an' see if they've got anything we need.'

Abbie exploded. 'Mr Curtis!' she cried. 'Don't you think it was bad enough that I had to kill these two men to protect myself. Now you want me to rob their bodies. Don't be such a ghoul.'

Abbie, considerably upset by the killings and all that had happened to her in the last few days, went into a tirade about her experiences in America and how she wished that she had never left England. She paused to draw breath and finally, half sobbing, burst out with, 'And don't ever call me girlie. I've a name. Abigail! Or, if you wish Abbie! But most certainly not girlie!'

Billy Curtis was startled by her passionate outburst and was immediately crestfallen. 'Aw! Don't take on so, gir – I

29

mean, Abbie. It's jus' that we can't leave 'em here with their guns an' stuff. Look at the sky! It won't be long before them there buzzards will be bringin' other folks here. An' the chances are they'll be Injuns. We've gotta get out of here quick.'

Abbie quickly glanced at the sky where already a dozen carrion-seekers were wheeling and circling high overhead, brought by some mysterious process to the place of death. Stifling her repugnance, she bent and relieved Jake's corpse of a double-barrelled pistol and a military musket engraved with a stamped US and an American eagle. His companion had carried a rusted single-barrelled shotgun of a large bore – probably of Belgian origin. The piece looked as if it would have been more dangerous to the shooter than to any would-be target.

The three guns were handed to Billy who stowed them alongside in the travois. That was the limit of Abbie's corpse-searching, although she did acknowledge the need to take the two horses belonging to the dead men. It was that or unsaddle them and leave them to hopefully be found wandering and grazing. She tied the Mexican's horse alongside her bay and, reluctantly mounting that of the late Jake, she led the little expedition westward at a steady clip that bounced Billy up and down and at times threatened to toss him off the travois. His cries for her to slow down were ignored. Abbie was relentless in her intent to put as many miles as possible between themselves and the two corpses.

Eventually Billy insisted that they halt in the cover of a rocky outcrop. 'Abbie!' he cried. 'This here way of travelling jus' won't work! I think that I could probably ride ol' Jake's horse iffen you'd help me up on him. Least it'd be more practical than that there contraption you've got balanced atop of your bay'. He cast a disgusted look at Abbie's English, expensively-constructed side-saddle, custom-built for ladies of quality. 'I sure couldn't see my way clear to perch up on that thing.'

Abbie ignored his remarks and, pursing her lips a trifle, she dismounted and proceeded to unlash the improvised harness that secured the travois to the bay. This done, under Billy's direction she turned the Mexican's horse into a pack-animal, bearing her plunder, Billy's belongings and the extra guns taken from the two bad eggs.

She assisted Billy to mount, with one splint-bound leg sticking strangely out to one side and, when he was comfortable, climbed aboard her own horse and they continued their strange journey westward. Now Billy led the way, deliberately going for long periods over ground that would leave little or no trace of their passage. Without the travois their tracks were much reduced and they made more satisfactory progress. The terrain was gradually changing as the rolling endless prairies gave way to more and more outcrops of rocks, indicating the start of the foothills of the Rocky Mountains.

Although he made no comments, Billy was concerned about two problems that would have to be resolved. First of all there was a cold bite in the air and he knew that any day now they could expect snow, for which they were totally unprepared. At least Abbie was. He knew enough to cope with all weather conditions. At least he could if it wasn't for his broken leg.

31

The second issue which was gnawing at him was the possibility of pursuit by Cad Williams, the third member of Jake's gang. By this time he would have had time to reach a settlement and recruit some equally evil-minded characters only too willing to give chase to a hapless old man and assault a pretty young girl who somehow had been lucky in getting off two mortal shots. Cad would want revenge!

'Hold up Abbie!' Sitting awkwardly in the saddle, Billy Curtis described his concerns to Abbie and proposed that they head north for his cabin where he could lay up until his leg was healed. He had already provisioned the place against the coming winter and there was more than enough for two.

Furthermore he reckoned that he could create some more suitable apparel for his female companion from his tanned deer-hides. Billy pointed out that while he was incapacitated by his broken leg, Abbie's assistance would be invaluable, while he in turn could equip her with some frontier clothing and also teach her how to survive in the West.

Abbie was not long in agreeing with Billy's proposal. Being alone and very conscious of all the unknown issues that she was likely to encounter if by herself, she was secretly grateful that these subjects had been raised. Therefore they turned their horses north towards Billy's hidden cabin.

As they rode, Billy described his life growing up on the frontier, especially after his Tennessean folks were killed in an Indian raid. He, as a mere nine-year-old, had gone off fishing in a distant creek and had thereby avoided the dawn attack which for a short time became known as the

'Curtis Massacre'.

Neighbours who arrived too late to aid the unfortunate family found the small boy wandering close to the smoking ruins of his cabin and futilely attempting to bury his scalped parents and two siblings.

One of his neighbours, a bachelor, had taken the dry-eyed lad and promised to give him a good home, but Billy soon found his promises were worthless, being made to work from daybreak to long after nightfall, expected to eat scraps, wear cast-off clothing and sleep on sacking in the lean-to which housed the man's animals.

Billy had endured this slavery for nearly two years and had then taken off and commenced fending for himself. Over the years he had swamped out saloons, mucked out pigsties and done all manner of odd jobs that could be done by a small boy. Later he'd worked in a logging camp, mined unsuccessfully for gold and silver, herded cattle down on the Texas plains and spent years trapping and trading for furs with various Indian tribes.

He spoke familiarly of names that at that time meant very little to Abbie, who had never been introduced to the exploits of Jim Bridger, Kit Carson or even Davy Crockett. However, she listened politely and, whenever Billie paused, she attempted to give him some idea of her own upbringing. It was an uphill task. Although Billy could read, after a fashion, he had very little notion of life on the American eastern seaboard, let alone life across the ocean in England. Her attempts to describe life in India amid the ordered routine of a British regiment, or the native life of the local population, were met with smiles of disbelief. The only time Abbie perceived a spark of true interest was

33

when she described the hunting trips with her father and how she had learned to shoot. Then she found that they had a common topic of interest.

CHAPTER FOUR

Their route was now north-west, with the rising hills broken up into a confusing mixture of valleys and blind canyons. To the cottonwoods along the creeks was added a growing variety of deciduous trees, such as aspen and birch, while conifers were to be seen on the lower reaches of the rocky hills.

Billy urged his horse into a narrow arroyo down which trickled a fast-running stream. Ahead the way appeared blocked by a huge granite boulder, but the old trapper led his steed into the bushes to the right of the blockage. As he pushed his way through, Abbie, following closely, noticed the barest trace of a trail indicating that this pathway had been used before.

The rocks on either side closed in so that she could barely make out the grey-blue sky overhead, and in the narrow cleft it would have been possible to touch the rocky walls either side by raising her arms. After a short distance the cleft widened and the light increased, suggesting that the narrow stifling rockbound trail was ending, and shortly thereafter the expedition emerged into a deep basin completely surrounded by high cliffs.

This hidden valley was possibly a quarter of a mile long, by four hundred yards in width, with the same stream she had seen earlier trickling merrily across the grass-covered centre of the basin, and vanishing into the rocks at the base of the towering cliffs. Halfway down the valley Billy had built his cabin using, from the evidence of the many stumps projecting from the grass, the trees to be found in the basin.

The cabin was nestled right up against the base of a lofty crag, and the grey weathered appearance of its squared-off logs blended well against the rocky background. There was a short hitching rail in front at which Abbie tied their horses and then helped Billy to dismount. Steadying himself on Abbie's shoulder, Billy hopped to his cabin and, unlatching the door, invited his young companion to enter.

Abbie did so and stared around curiously. She found herself in a room about eighteen feet long, and twelve feet wide, with a stone fireplace at one end. On the front wall, either side of the centrally placed door, were two small, glassed windows which gave but limited daylight to the room. There was a roughly made table and two stools and, at the opposite end to the fireplace, there was a built-in bunk.

Apart from a few pegs and two or three shelves, upon which she was surprised to note there stood several books, the cabin appeared to be bare.

Billy had sunk down exhausted upon one of the stools

and, looking up, saw the look of dismay on Abbie's face. 'Don't you worry yourself, Miss Abbie. You'll have your female privacy. Take a peep through the doorway, behind yonder blanket.'

Abbie crossed the room to the hitherto unnoticed Hudson's Bay blanket hanging on the far wall, and pulled it to one side. Beyond, to her left, was a small room, complete with bunk, receiving daylight by, of all things, a ship's porthole that had been cleverly built into the wall. Across from her quarters was a storeroom, behind which was a shallow cave containing yet more supplies. Billy had not exaggerated when he had stated that he was stocked up for winter.

Abbie Penraven stood at the open door of Billy's cabin enjoying the unaccustomed warmth of the southern spring breeze which was rapidly melting the snow in the hidden valley. This was hardly the same young women who had entered the rocky basin in her scant and bedraggled attire the previous Fall.

This Abbie was a brown, sun- and wind-tanned figure with strong, hard, calloused hands revealing that she had been engaged in many forms of manual labour. Her light brown hair was cropped unfashionably short and merely tied at the back with a piece of rawhide, and her handsome features required no artificial aids to enhance her natural beauty.

She was clad in a buckskin shirt that came down almost to her knees, and her legs were covered in a pair of soft leather pants that, like her upper garment, were fringed down the sides. On her feet were moccasin-like boots, with solid soles and heels and soft uppers, into which her pants were tucked.

Around her waist was slung a broad leather belt from which hung on the left hand, cross-draw position, a holster in which reposed her pinfire revolver. This rig was balanced by a ten-inch Bowie knife resting just below her right hip.

The winter months had been a learning revelation to Abbie. Because of Billy's broken leg, for quite some time most of the chores had fallen upon her shoulders, and in doing them she had by force of circumstances acquired a number of new skills. Under Billy's directions she had done most of the cooking which, after some disastrous failures, began to produce quite palatable meals. The making of hot biscuits, sourdough and otherwise, were her first successful accomplishment.

Although Billy had laid in a large quantity of logs against the forthcoming winter, these had to be split and stacked inside, drying close to the stone fireplace, whilst others were piled against the outside walls. Yet more wood in the shape of tree trunks, which had been felled the previous year, had to be hauled and skidded from other scattered locations in the valley using the horses for haulage. And, of course, the animals had to be attended to.

Forty yards from the cabin along the cliff face was a large cave and, in front of this, Billy had erected a corral so that the animals could exercise in the enclosed area yet, in inclement weather, could seek shelter in the cave. For fodder he had accumulated a large supply of hay cut from the grass, and this was supplemented with grain from his stores.

Initially Abbie had staggered to her room and had flopped down on her bed absolutely exhausted, but in time her muscles hardened. The many tasks grew easier with repeated use and she was able to take her ease at various times of the day. And of course as Billy's broken leg gradually healed, he too was able to share the load of chores required to survive their winter of isolation.

With more leisure time, Abbie examined the books lying on the shelf adjacent to the fireplace and was both surprised and delighted to discover several novels of Sir Walter Scott and one by Charles Dickens. Billy, like most Westerners, had a great respect for the written word and, although but a poor reader himself, had willingly taken these volumes in trade when the opportunity arose. He therefore was equally pleased to learn that Abbie was an accomplished scholar and not only could help him to read but would willingly read out loud to him during the long dark winter evenings.

In return for Abbie's aid, Billy helped her convert some of the well-cured deer hides into the serviceable apparel that she wore on that spring morning. It was also Billy who fashioned a suitable holster for her pinfire revolver and, having presented his gift to her and seen her pistol nestled in place, stated, 'Now we've gotta make sure that you can pull that shootin' iron quickly an' hit yer target every time.'

Abbie protested that she knew how to shoot and cited the episode resulting in Jake's demise, but Billy merely shook his head. 'You was darned lucky, Abbie. Ol' Jake jus' never thought that any she-male would be carrying an

39

equalizer, so you had the drop on him. Next time it could be different.'

Eventually Abbie allowed herself to be persuaded that she needed lessons in western-style pistol lore and her instruction began. Billy had decided that, because of her small stature and the size and weight of her pistol, she should continue to use the two-handed grip with which she was familiar, but he had her practise continually so that her draw became a fluid movement as she pulled and cocked her revolver while aiming at a mark on the cabin's wall.

When he was satisfied, Billy decided that she must progress to live firing, but to save her pinfire cartridges, the shooting would be done using the single shot 'chimney piece' that was supplied by the pistol's maker. A square of birch bark about the size of an adult hand was tacked to the far wall of the cabin and the chimney piece, loaded with powder and ball, was inserted in an empty chamber. The other chambers were left empty. When the chimney was capped with a percussion cap, Abbie re-holstered her pistol and stood hands at her sides facing the far wall. Billy suddenly called, 'Draw!' and Abbie, crouching slightly, drew and fired at the white target. There was a flash and a boom and the cabin was filled with white greyish smoke reeking of bad eggs. As the smoke cleared, Abbie ran forward to examine the result of her shot. She was disappointed to see that she had just clipped the edge of the birch bark. Billy, on the other hand, was impressed with the first attempt of his pupil and encouraged her to try again, and yet again, as the winter months passed until, by the time that Spring arrived, he was confident that Abbie Penraven could face and probably out-gun any of the bad characters she was likely to encounter in her travels westward.

CHAPTER FIVE

Abbie turned back into the cabin. 'Billy!' she announced, 'spring has finally arrived. It's time to get moving.'

Billy looked up from the leatherwork in which he was currently engaged. 'Yep, I figured that sunshine would get your feet itchin'. I'll get my plunder together.' He rose from his stool and then paused as Abbie raised a hand as though to restrain him.

'No, Billy! You sit tight. This is one journey I'll be making alone. You've done enough for me. I have to stand on my own and give you a chance to fully recover from your encounter with that old grizzly last year.' In vain Billy protested that he was fine, in fact was as fit as when he was a boy of twenty.

Abbie smiled at this boast, but was adamant. She had watched the old trapper while they were doing some of the many tasks in the hidden valley and had seen with concern how he would frequently have to rest while engaged in a relatively simple job, which at one time had been child's play for him. She, therefore, was insistent that the journey westward was one which she would have to take alone.

However, she was far from averse to accept Billy's aid when packing supplies and deciding what she would need and what should be taken. A supply of jerky from a deer brought down by her own skills, flour, sugar, coffee, a quantity of salt ladled from Billy's ample stocks into small linen bags, and three or four pounds of bacon constituted her food supplies. Her clothing was her buckskins, and the red velvet riding habit, dried and carefully hung up, but unworn since the attack on the wagon train. Now the habit was bundled together with some homemade small clothing into a canvas sack in lieu of a carpet bag.

For defence Abbie had her pinfire revolver and the Bowie knife. She insisted that these were sufficient, but Billy was not so sure. 'Abbie, girl! If you have to face either hostile Injuns or white trash like them we met up with on the trail, you're gonna need a long gun. Keep 'em off at ta distance, that's what I say.'

He went to his storeroom and returned with the rifle taken from the corpse of the violently deceased Jake. 'Here y'are! Thought that this'd come in useful sometime. Military Springfield, 'bout ten years old, I'd figure. 'Bout .58 calibre. Just what you need.'

He handed the weapon to Abbie who took it reluctantly, with thoughts of how she had come to possess it. But she was sufficiently realistic to accept the fact that Billy was right. She did need a firearm with long range capability. But the old trapper wasn't quite finished.

' 'Scuse me, Abbie, I think you need a belly. . . .' He

43

stopped, aghast at the outraged look on the English girl's face, 'Er, what I mean is, you need an equalizer, a hide-out gun, 'case you bin relieved of your pinfire.' He hastened to explain that such a hidden weapon was frequently described as a belly gun, since it was concealed against the stomach, behind the owner's belt.

Billy thought for a moment and then rummaged among the packs in the storeroom. 'Hah!' he exclaimed triumphantly, 'How about this little beauty?'

He came back flourishing a small cap and ball revolver. 'Here y'are, Abbie! Jus' the thing for you.' So saying, he handed her a Colt .31 caliber, 1849 model, in seemingly pristine condition.

'Billy, where did you obtain such a pistol? You didn't. . . .' She left the rest of her sentence unsaid as she turned the pistol over in her hands.

Billy realized what she was implying and hastened to explain that he had come across a dying man some years back, a gambler by the cut of his clothes, and the man had given him the gun in gratitude for having eased his last hours. 'So you see, Abbie, it's mine, all legal-like, an' I hereby give it to you!'

Two days later Abbie, astride her bay and leading a roan as a packhorse, made her departure from Billy's hidden valley. Tucked under her buckskin shirt, and held securely inside her waistband, nestled Billy's gift resting a trifle uncomfortably against her stomach. Common sense had dictated that she use a man's saddle rather than the elegant but impractical English side-saddle that she had been using when she first encountered the injured trapper. Billy had advised and shown Abbie how to efficiently pack her spare clothing; food and utensils into balanced loads secured by diamond hitches on either side of the docile roan.

Farewells had been brief. Abbie felt a lump in her throat as, seated in her saddle, she had looked down affectionately at Billy who stood with one hand holding her horse's halter.

'Well, Abbie, you'd better git afore you change your mind,' he had exclaimed gruffly while wiping away what he said was a speck of dirt from his eye. 'So long, partner!' And with a slap at the bay's rump he turned back into the cabin.

'Goodbye, Billy! I'll always be thinking about you!'

So saying she had dug her heels into the bay's flanks and, resisting the temptation to look back, had rode off on her lonely quest.

Cautiously she rode through the narrow cleft, very conscious of the clip-clopping of her animals' hoofs echoing and re-echoing from the rocky faces on either side. Leaving both horses at the entrance to the cleft, Abbie slipped noiselessly through the bushes and peered out down the narrow arroyo. All was still, apart from the gurgling of the little stream, and there were no signs of any human activity. So collecting her animals, she mounted and rode forth, following carefully the detailed instructions that Billy had given her on how to link up with the westbound trail.

Abbie obeyed the old trapper's advice to the letter, keeping carefully below the skyline wherever possible and exercising extra caution whenever she approached any outcrops of rocks or isolated groves of trees, either of which could conceal potential enemies. So she rode, ceaselessly swivelling her head to note the terrain through which she travelled. It would be easy to be distracted by all the welcome signs of the western spring. The prairie was a riot of colour created by thousands of flowers. The few trees offered inviting shade with their bright, green foliage, and the jack rabbits and prairie dogs constantly sought to distract her with their antics. But the English girl ignored all the distractions, especially the temptation to use her long gun and add to her provisions by shooting one of the whitetail deer that were placidly grazing and ignoring the passing of the horses and their solitary rider.

Abbie's route was roughly south-west and by late afternoon, as the sun sank towards the jagged peaks of the foothills of the Rocky Mountains, she encountered the first indication that others had passed that way. The ground was scored and rutted by the wheels of countless wagons and, by the side of the trail, there was the pitiful remnant of one such vehicle, a broken wheel and a few pieces of half burnt timber, the mute evidence of what had probably once been somebody's hopes and ambitions. Close by there were three low mounds of soil, indicating the last resting place of the wagon's occupants. Even as she passed, Abbie noted that the relentless prairie wind was busy levelling the grave sites. Soon there would be nothing to show the passer-by the location. Abbie shivered and urged her mount away from the spot.

Shortly thereafter, Abbie turned off the trail and found a sheltered place where she cooked a hurried meal over a small, smokeless fire. Bacon and a bannock, washed down with a mug of black, sugarless coffee, was her lonely repast. Then after cleaning her utensils and removing traces of the fire, Abbie remounted and, obeying Billy's teaching, rode on a good mile or so before finding a concealed place where she bedded down for the night, after first hobbling her horses to ensure that they would not stray.

Through the night she dozed fitfully, huddled under her blanket, head pillowed on her saddle and right hand firmly grasping the pinfire pistol. The one sound almost constantly heard was the noise of the horses pulling at the grass with their strong teeth as they grazed. This comforting background noise was periodically punctuated by the howl of some lone coyote serenading the moon and causing Abbie to startle into full consciousness. After each alert it was some time before she once more slipped into a shallow sleep.

All in all, Abbie had a restless night, and got up shivering in the cold morning air, noting a heavy wet dew covering all her possessions and glistening off the grass and bushes. Ruefully, she reflected that the lonely night had been of her own choosing since Billy had been quite prepared to accompany her. She shrugged her shoulders philosophically and, bringing to mind a half-remembered quotation from her schooldays, resolved to 'stiffen up her sinews' and 'quicken the blood', especially the latter, and get a fire going with which to prepare breakfast.

The sun was just peeping above the eastern horizon by the time she had breakfasted, performed a hurried ablution, packed her gear, caught and saddled the bay and loaded the docile roan. With a last look around her camp-site to ensure that there was little evidence of her stay, Abbie mounted her horse and headed once more towards the west.

CHAPTER SIX

After three days of such uneventful progress, with no sign of any other humans, white or otherwise, Abbie was relieved to see wisps of smoke arising from a cluster of buildings straddling the trail some distance ahead. An optimistic sign, painted on a sagging board to her left, told the passing wayfarer that she was approaching the town of Paradise.

Drawing closer, she noted that this budding metropolis consisted of a number of weather-beaten, unpainted, wooden shacks placed haphazardly either side of the wheel-rutted path that led through Paradise. To her right was a corral, attached to a barn in a sad state of disrepair, and a sign above the open doorway indicated that this was 'McCain's Livery and Feed'. The proprietor himself called out a friendly 'Howdy, stranger!' as Abbie passed, no doubt hoping that the young rider in buckskins might prove to be a potential customer. Abbie just waved her right hand in salutation as she pulled up in front of a larger false-fronted building, which announced to the passing world that this was 'Charlie Kunz General Store and Saloon'. In smaller letters below was daubed the claim that Charlie offered 'The Best Food in Town!', which, considering the dearth of possible competition, was more than a trifle pretentious!

Abbie sat for a few moments, looking at the sign and ignoring the curious gazes from a trio of be-whiskered local gentry seated on the boardwalk. She didn't really need any further supplies, although some extra fine powder for the .31 calibre Colt might be useful. Billy had given her enough to make up about twenty loads, but that didn't leave much available for practice. In addition, a store-cooked meal might be a change from her own culinary fare. Making up her mind, Abbie slipped from the saddle and, securing both of her horses to the rail in loose 'getaway' hitches, she pushed through the batwing doors and entered Mr Kunz's establishment.

She paused inside the doorway, to allow her eyes to become accustomed to the relative gloom of the interior after the glare of the noon-day sun. Facing her was the bar, a solid slab of some hardwood, resting on the tops of two large barrels. Behind the bar, against the rear wall, was a shelf with a number of dubious-looking bottles offering alcoholic solace to the desperate and unwary customer. To the left was piled along another counter the products offered in the 'General Store', consisting of blankets, range clothing and leather boots sharing most of the space with a limited number of hand farm implements, while a rack of assorted rifles and shotguns took up space between the two grimy-paned windows that reluctantly provided some natural lighting. To the right a couple of roughly-made tables and chairs suggested that this was the dining area.

As Abbie entered the establishment, the solitary occupant, ensconced behind the bar, called out a hearty 'Howdy, young fella!' while at the same time industriously polishing the none-too-clean bar counter with a less-than-white bar cloth. 'What'll it be?' His small twinkling eyes opened wide as he noted his error in identification. 'Sorry, ma'am. I guess I haf made a big mistake! Whatcha doin' in dat outfit?' His abject apology was delivered in a warm guttural tone denoting his Germanic ancestry.

Abbie smiled at his confusion. 'That is perfectly all right, Mr Kunz. I can appreciate your error. It's just that this clothing is far more comfortable and suitable for travelling than any female attire.' Her explanation was given in a clear, modulated, English accent so at odds with her rough frontier appearance, causing the bartender's jaw to drop open in surprise and confusion.

'Vat can I for you do? Ve can't serve you at de bar, but. . . .'

He broke off as Abbie smilingly shook her head. 'No, Mr Kunz! I was not seeking liquid refreshment, but perhaps I could purchase a lunch from you?'

'Oh, *ja*! Dat is OK. *Mein Frau* is von good cook. So de men tell me.' He chuckled at his little joke and went on to explain, apologetically, that his lunchtime fare was very limited, neglecting to mention that the same limited dishes were offered from early morning to late at night. The meal would consist of fried venison, beans, hot biscuits and coffee.

Abbie indicated that his offering would be perfectly acceptable, and crossed to one of the tables while mine

51

host shouted the order through a doorway back into a lean-to kitchen. A muffled female voice indicated that the culinary preparations were underway and, shortly after much male and female whispering in the kitchen, Abbie was presented with a chipped mug of steaming black coffee. Less than five minutes later the short plump figure of *Frau* Kunz appeared, a broad smile on her heat-reddened face, framed by two long blonde plaits. She bore dishes and silverware that initially were placed upon the bar, while she spread a small white cloth on Abbie's table. Then the dishes were transferred to the table. Abbie found before her a plate of thinly sliced, fried venison, a large bowl of beans, swimming in a tomato-based sauce, and a small pyramid of hot biscuits, together with the cutlery with which to consume the appetizing meal. At gestures from the smiling German couple, Abbie willingly demolished the food laid before her and had barely finished her second cup of coffee when the pleasant interlude came to an abrupt end.

Directly Abbie had entered the Kunz Emporium, the trio on the sidewalk, joined by half a dozen other curious citizens of Paradise, had surrounded Abbie's two horses, eyeing their good points, their harness and above all their brands. One individual had then set off in a shambling run to a tumbledown shack at the western end of the built-up area. Abbie was paying her bill for the food and complimenting the hospitable couple, when the batwing doors were thrust violently open and several men appeared.

'Yeah, that's her! That's the one who murdered my two pards in cold blood!'

Abbie was suddenly confronted with the hate-filled visage of Cad Williams, whom she'd last seen riding off to the east with his hands held high above his head, now standing twelve feet from her, one hand on a pistol, while the forefinger of the left hand was pointed accusingly at her.

'Shot poor ol' Jake down in cold blood, an' then killed Pedro Gonzalez! Two of the most gentle men as ever walked the earth!' As Cad cried out these accusations, even some of the cronies in his wake looked dubious at what sounded less than truth. The man who had summoned Williams attempted to back him up.

'She's nothin' more than a dirty lil' horse thief! An' we all know how to handle horse stealers! String her up!'

His suggestion was echoed by a couple of the other intruders less concerned with the truth of Cad William's accusations than with the novel idea of watching a victim, a woman at that, swinging in her death agonies from the hoist above the door of the livery stable.

'Hold it, boys! Ve ain't havin' no necktie party here, vith no trial!' All turned towards the bar where Charlie Kunz the owner stood, covering the crowd with a ten gauge shotgun clutched tightly in his pudgy hands. 'Let's see vat der young lady has to say for herself.'

He nodded to Abbie who spoke, hesitantly at first, but whose voice became louder and more precise as she continued, outlining some of the events that had led to the encounter with Jake and his gang. She briefly described the attack on the wagon train, her finding of Billy Curtis, his injuries and their joint attempts to travel west with the travois.

At the mention of Billy's name there was a subtle change in the attitude of the listeners. Hitherto, most of them had heard her story with semi-polite disbelief, and with frequent negative comments. However, many of them knew, or knew of, the old mountain man, and Abbie's story began to have a ring of truth about it. She finished the tale of her decision to travel westward, and the reason why she had declined Billy's aid, and it was by then evident that the vast majority of her listeners were fully convinced that she had told the truth.

Dark looks were cast towards Cad Williams and his chief crony. Unfortunately, rather than quietly allowing that they were in error, the pair chose to curse and bluster and demand their notion of justice. Seeing that the crowd had dismissed the accusations against the girl, Cad lost complete control and, with a foul oath, and a cry of, 'She ain't gonna live to tell that tale again!' he pulled a pepperbox revolver from a belt holster.

Abbie had been watching him intently, alert for any hostile action and, as Cad drew his pistol, she acted just as she had practised all winter long in the cabin. Dropping to a crouch, she half turned to the right while simultaneously reaching for, and drawing, her pinfire pistol. Her left hand automatically locked into position forward of the trigger-guard, as her left thumb found and cocked her piece. Cad Williams was still bringing his cumbersome gun up to the firing position when Abbie fired her first shot. At the last second she disobeyed Billy's oft-repeated dictum: 'Always go for the gut or the chest,' and she put a 12mm bullet in

Williams' shoulder. He yelped as he dropped his pistol, but reached for a wicked-looking Arkansas Toothpick in his left boot. Reluctantly, Abbie fired once more and then yet again; this time they were heart shots. Cad Williams slumped to the floor. The crowd stood frozen at the sudden gunplay, and Abbie Penraven stood there, pistol in hand, wreathed in a widening pall of grey smoke. Though not on the road to Damascus, Cad Williams' chief crony had a similar startling conversion. Muttering that he had made a terrible mistake, he departed and vanished from Abbie's life.

Despite Abbie's original intentions, she accepted a pressing invitation to spend the night in Paradise. Charlie Kunz showed her a small storeroom behind the bar, where she could bed down and feel secure, with a strong bolt on the door. With her saddle and pack stashed in the room and both horses in McCain's livery stable, Abbie, in truth, was relieved that she did not have to face the lonely trail so soon after being forced to shoot a man, even if he did richly deserve to die.

After an evening meal, which was very similar to that which she had consumed at midday, she had been heartily glad to retire to her little room and sink down on the single bed, both mentally and physically worn out. Beyond the door she could still hear the men at the bar loudly reliving every second of her gunfight with Cad Williams and comparing notes with other gunplay they had observed, or about which they had heard. Two aspects continually came to the fore in loud and excited conversation. The first was the speed with which Abbie had drawn and, secondly, the accuracy of her shots. Strangely, only one had remarked upon the breech-loading pinfire pistol she was packing, and he referred to her as 'the pinfire lady'. It was a description that she was to hear time and time again. Abbie finally fell asleep lulled by the murmur of male voices in the saloon, yet very disturbed that, within the last few months, she had shot and killed three men, and seemed to have acquired a somewhat unsavoury reputation.

CHAPTER SEVEN

The following morning, while drinking a welcome cup of coffee, a shadow fell across her table.

'S'cuse me, lady. Could I ask a question of you?' Abbie indicated her permission with a slight nod of her head.

'You're heading west, I 'ear. Would it be possible to travel wiv' you as far as the settlement on the South Platte River, Colorado Territory? I'd be no trouble!' he hastened to say. 'And I got me own vittles. It's just more comfortable for a body 'aving someone along who knows 'ow to 'andle themselves.'

Abbie looked more closely at the owner of the part Cockney, part European, voice standing before her. She saw a small, hardly more than five feet tall, man regarding her with a pleading look in his eyes. His brown face and rather greasy long side-locks led her to surmise that her petitioner was possibly a gypsy, or more probably Jewish.

The latter assumption turned out to be correct. Jacob Levy, for such was his name, was originally from Poland, but his parents had fled during one of the Russian-inspired pogroms to London, England, where he had been raised in the Jewish community of Whitechapel. Later, seeking his fortune, he had emigrated to the United States and had wandered westward as a pedlar, selling pins, needles, and all sorts of gewgaws to isolated homesteads along the way.

Abbie didn't really want to be a shepherdess to anyone seemingly incapable of looking out for themselves and so she probed a little deeper. Jacob had been on a small wagon train, but several members of the party had been increasingly vocal in stating that every stroke of bad luck they experienced was due to the fact that they had this 'dirty Jew', like an albatross hanging around their necks. Finally, his situation got so bad that Jacob with his one-horse trap had pulled out of the wagon train when it reached Paradise, and there he had remained, unable to attach himself to any respectable party travelling west.

While Abbie sat pondering Jacob Levy's request, another man, with a young woman in tow, approached her table. Abbie looked up enquiringly at this latest interruption.

'Permission to speak, ma'am?'

Facing her was a bluff, red-faced man, probably in his mid-forties, who stood stiff as a ramrod, feet together at forty-five degrees, and hands held rigidly at his sides. Abbie noted with more than a little curiosity that she was being addressed by somebody who had definitely experienced military service.

'Jack Harding, ma'am, late corporal in the 44th Regiment of Foot; honourably discharged from the garrison of Fort Henry, Kingston in Upper Canada. This 'ere's me wife Polly. We've been properly married these last three years. Polly's family in Toronto died of the cholera outbreak. We've been making our way west, and wondered if we could join your party?' Harding's information and request was delivered in the nature of a military report and Abbie looked at the ex-soldier with interest.

'Discharged soldier, eh? Can you shoot, corporal?'

Jack puffed up with pride at her use of his old military rank, but corrected her gently. 'Not corporal any more, miss. Just Mr Harding, if you please. Yes, I can shoot. I 'ad me Crossed Rifles badge,' thus indicating that he had been qualified as a marksman in the regiment. 'I've got me own rifle too, miss. Bought it as surplus to requirements.'

He produced a British-made weapon upon which Abbie looked with fond memories.

'Why, that's an Enfield! I used one in Kashmir years ago!'

Jack Harding had been stationed in India and, for several moments, the two of them were lost in a welter of memories of depots and cantonments in the sub-continent. A polite cough brought them back to reality where Jacob Levy was still awaiting a reply to his plea.

Abbie quickly made up her mind. 'Why yes, Mr Levy. I would be delighted to have you accompany us.' Her use of the royal plural not only told Jacob that he was acceptable but also informed both Jack and Polly Harding that they would be welcome. Polly it seemed had once lived on a backwoods farm north of Toronto and was familiar with a shotgun. Jacob, on the other hand, was a complete novice where firearms were concerned, although Jack Harding stressed that he would soon rectify that lack in

Mr Levy's education.

'There are two things upon which I insist. First of all, you, Mr Levy and you, Polly, must obtain firearms that you can handle. Mr Harding, perhaps you could assist with their selection.'

Jack Harding nodded. Abbie paused and, looking at her prospective travelling companions, assumed a stern expression: 'You people are joining me. I am not joining you! I will be the captain of this party, and I expect you to follow my instructions!'

Three days later Abbie Penraven's little command had more than doubled in size. The first two days had been uneventful. They had set off early in the morning after bidding farewells to Mr and Mrs Kunz and the other folk of Paradise who wished them well on their journey to the west. They travelled with the Harding wagon in front, followed by Jacob Levy's two-wheeled cart, behind which was hitched Abbie's roan packhorse, leaving her free to roam ahead astride the bay.

On the afternoon of the third day, a small cluster of wagons was to be seen half a mile to the south of the main trail. Calling a halt, Abbie rode cautiously over to see who the strangers were, and why they were circled rather than travelling at that time of day. As she approached, a young lad of possibly fifteen or sixteen years, clutching a double-barrelled shotgun, ordered her to halt and state her business.

'My name is Penraven and I'm guiding the wagons you can see to your north. What's the problem here?'

The shotgun was lowered and Abbie was permitted to

enter the enclosure created by the five wagons. Immediately, she was surrounded by a group of women, all talking at once, while an old, grey-bearded man sat on a wagon tongue and shook his head slowly from side to side. Abbie took a deep breath and raised her voice.

'Quiet!' she roared in a voice that would have pleased Company Sergeant Major Jones. 'Be quiet all of you! Now one person and one only please, tell me what is going on here?'

The women gradually fell silent, looking at each other and at the buckskin clad girl, holstered pistol at her hip, who sat looking down upon them. Finally, a middle-aged member of the little group pushed herself forward and said, 'Well, miss.' She paused, took a deep breath and then proceeded to describe the tale of their dire fortune. They had left Independence as part of a fourteen-vehicle wagon train bound for Santa Fe. Just before they reached the cut-off for the Mountain Division trail that led to the north-west, a party of excited men came up from behind. Over the evening campfires they told of literally mountains of gold to be had in the Colorado Territory. Apparently, fresh discoveries were being made every day. The strangers moved on the following morning and left the wagon train seething with arguments like an overturned beehive.

Some were saying they should head north-west, others that they should stick with the trail to Santa Fe. Eventually, the train split, eight continuing on their original course, and six determined to seek their fortunes in the gold fields. The smaller party had been led by her husband Jeb Marlowe, who, though not a scout, was a reasonably good

61

frontiersman. Unfortunately, shortly after the wagon train split, his horse fell on him, shattering his left leg and, shortly thereafter, gangrene set in. He had lingered for a week and finally died leaving the group leaderless.

One wagon broke down and had to be abandoned, its contents distributed among the remaining five. Then they had Indian trouble. A group of warriors rode up and demanded horses, guns and whiskey. Upon being questioned, Mrs Marlowe admitted that though person- ally she had not seen any war-paint, the men, convinced that they had to act quickly, opened fire on the braves. Two fell, the others rode off and four of the men rode hotly in pursuit. They had not returned and had been missing for a full week. Therefore, the only males left in the party were fifteen-year-old Bobby Smith and the elderly man, Mark Isaacson, seated on the wagon tongue.

'We can't stay here, miss. If our men do manage to get free of those red devils, they could follow our trail, if we left a message on a board or something, Would it be pos- sible for us to join up with y'all?'

The other women nodded in agreement to her plea, and Abbie realized that they had already had the notion of getting to a safer location before she had appeared on the scene.

Abbie looked around the campsite; the women stared back hopefully. She was reluctant to take on the added responsibility, but seemed to have no choice. 'Very well. Now how many drovers can you muster between you?'

The women looked at each other and again it was Ann Marlowe who appointed herself spokeswoman.

'Miss, I can drive my own wagon. Jeb an' I always shared the work.'

Beth Isaacson volunteered the fact that she thought she could handle their team with her husband doing some of the more simple tasks. She added that he had not been right in the head since their son Tom had ridden off after the Indians.

Bobby Smith spoke up stating that he and his mom could handle their outfit and this was followed by two more women, Naomi Johnson and Eve Schultz now sharing a wagon, indicating that they thought they could manage their rig between them.

The group turned and looked at their unspoken member. Dora McAdam stared back defiantly. Abbie looked with great interest at this remaining member of the stranded wagon train. She saw a well-dressed girl of about her own age, with blonde hair peeping out from her poke bonnet. She stood arms akimbo on her generous hips with her chin raised. 'Oh, you can all stare! You all think I'm incapable of doing anything except leading your men astray, but you're wrong! Yes, miss! I'll handle my own team, and I won't let you down!'

Abbie nodded with dubious satisfaction, suspecting that there had been problems among the distaff members of this wagon train. 'What guns have you got and how many know how to use them?'

The reply was far from encouraging. The only firearms left with the wagon train were Bobby Smith's shotgun, and a flintlock pistol owned by old Mr Isaacson. Unfortunately, the pistol also lacked a flint, which meant that currently it was useless. Proficiency with guns was practically non-existent.

'OK, people! Let's get those animals hitched up and everything prepared for moving!'

Abbie thought wryly, 'It's strange how I find myself tending to slip into Americanisms. Wouldn't Aunt Sarah be shocked! "OK", indeed! Next I'll be describing the animals as critters.'

With much confusion, and quite a number of loud, shrill, unladylike expletives, the women and Bobby slowly got their teams of oxen hitched to the wagons and prepared to move out, having left a brief message on a cleft stick in the centre of the campsite.

Abbie called out, 'Wagons roll!' and the move began. The Marlowe wagon was first, followed by the Isaacsons, with Beth walking alongside her team, brandishing a long whip, while Mr Isaacson sat placidly up on the seat loosely holding the reins. Next came Nelly Smith's outfit with young Bobby walking. Naomi and Eve seemed to work as a team as indeed they had for several weeks, and Dora McAdam brought up the rear, struggling tearfully to prove that she was as competent as the other women. Abbie meanwhile cantered back and forth along the length of the train, noting silently the many problems that hopefully would be cured by time.

When they neared the trail, she continued ahead and spoke to the Hardings waiting patiently in their wagon. 'We have other people joining us! Move ahead a mile or so and pick out a likely site for six or seven wagons. Make sure it has good water. Make camp there. The newcomers will get there eventually.' She fell back and passed the same instructions to Jacob Levy adding that there would be further explanations when they had made camp. Then Abbie rode back to where her new charges were manfully struggling to handle the lowing oxen.

When she reached the back of the column, she had a call from Dora McAdam, 'Miss Penraven, or do I call you captain?' Abbie noted a slightly mocking note in the query and responded sharply, 'Captain will do quite nicely, thank you. What do you want?'

Dora apologized for her slightly sarcastic remark and indicated that Abbie should climb up into the seat next to her. Curious, Abbie did as suggested, whereupon Dora elaborated about herself and the man with whom she had been travelling west. It was noted that there was no mention of marriage nor was Dora wearing a wedding ring. She had been working in a small store when Leonard Flynn had entered her life. He was a gambler and had just made a pile, or so he said. Dora, bored with the humdrum life of the store and an unhappy home situation, had jumped at the chance of a life of western adventure. Flynn promised her marriage and a good life, but she soon found out that his promises were like trying to hold on to quicksilver. They just slipped through one's fingers.

The main reason for speaking to Abbie was that the wagon contained a secret. She instructed her to check the boxes under the blankets. Abbie did so and was astonished to find that the boxes were stamped US Property. 'There's four boxes, and Flynn said that each one contained six rifles. That's twenty-four in all. They're stolen. Flynn said he'd skin me alive if I told anyone, but I figure he's probably dead himself now. Anyway, I know you could arm the whole wagon train with them,' she ended triumphantly.

Gradually the second portion of the wagon train reached the location that Jack Harding had chosen as a suitable campsite and the oxen were coaxed into turning so that the wagons were once more circled. Then the animals, both bovine and equine, were left to graze inside a rope corral. In no time campfires were alight as the women started preparing evening meals.

Abbie walked over to the Harding camp and asked Jack to step aside for a little chat. She told him about the contents of the McAdam wagon and of the need to get the women to the stage where they were reasonably proficient in the use of the rifles. 'Mr Harding, I'm hereby appointing you Sergeant of Arms. I want you to teach these women to shoot, and shoot accurately. Also I am going to state to all that, in my absence, you will be in command of the wagon train. Is this acceptable to you?'

Jack thought for a moment and then nodded. 'I'll do as you wish, ma'am, just as long as those women are prepared to accept my instructions, or orders. I won't stand for any nonsense.'

And so it was agreed and announced at a camp meeting later that evening. Initially, there was some giggling and smiling at the thought of being drilled by Jack Harding, but the women soon settled down to listen to the clear, concise explanations, especially as Abbie told them in no uncertain terms that their very lives might depend upon learning these new skills. It was aided by the fact that Jacob

Levy was only too glad to join the group to add to his admittedly meagre firearms knowledge.

Abbie was fairly satisfied with the progress that first evening and, since there was both powder and ball with the stolen weapons, was eager to let the women experience live shooting. She had also noted a certain sadness on the part of those who realized that they were now widows. They needed distraction, that is, all except for Dora McAdam who shed no tears over the loss of Len Flynn. However, if Abbie Penraven had had the wings of an eagle and had been able to soar high and see many miles from the trail, she would have been far from satisfied with the state of her wagon train.

CHAPTER EIGHT

When Len Flynn had left with the other men in pursuit of the Indians, he quite rapidly fell behind as his horse started limping. He had halted in a small grove of trees and had just removed a stone from his animal's left fore-hoof when he heard shooting up ahead. Cautiously he peered up the little valley from the undergrowth where he was hiding in time to see the end of the fight and view the ghastly scalping of his four companions.

Unable to retreat the way he had come, since he believed that yet more Indians blocked that way, he had been forced to go further and further from the wagon train until he was hopelessly lost amid the foothills of the mighty Rocky Mountains. And so he wandered for several days, existing on roots and a single jackrabbit that he managed to snare. Fear of the Indians prevented him from using his long gun to obtain larger game, and it was with initial relief that he met up with a party of white men.

His relief was very short-lived. An unkempt bunch of filthy, rag-garbed rogues, armed with an assortment of rusty guns and knives, surrounded him, fingering his clothing and possessions and disputing various items as though his throat was already slit. Thinking desperately of a means to save his life, Flynn cried out, 'Wait! Not too far from here I can show you a wagon train with just women there. It's yours for the taking, and one wagon is loaded with new rifles, far better than the junk you're using!'

The grim, one-eyed leader pushed the others aside and, stepping up close to the quaking Flynn, pressed a needle sharp Bowie against his victim's throat. 'They call me Scar. Now tell me that tale again.'

Flynn did so, mentally forgiving himself for betraying his late travelling companions. There was no other choice, he told himself. Another moment and he would have been a goner. For the moment he was alive.

His gun and knife were taken and, with hands tied in front of him, Flynn was permitted to sit and eat with the outlaw gang while they discussed ways of getting to this treasure trove of guns and women. Flynn rightly claimed that he was not at all sure of the location of the wagon train, but figured that it was still in the same location where he had left it, and so that's where the gang headed. Flynn was allowed to ride his own horse, but with a noose around his neck and the other end tied to the pommel of Scar's saddle.

Two days hard riding brought them to an area that Flynn thought he recognized. He was correct and later that morning they reached the location of the last campsite, bare of wagons but with a thick stick driven into the ground in the centre of the clearing. They dismounted. A folded note was resting in a split at the top of the stick. Flynn retrieved the note and reading it quickly passed it to the impatient Scar. He held it upside-down and demanded to know the contents. Ann Marlowe had scribbled the note very quickly and, since her scholastic achievements were limited, the note merely stated: 'Headed west with Inglish gurl on mane trayl.'

Flynn explained this move to Scar and his other captors. Scar said nothing while he pondered the contents of the message. 'So the wagons had been moved, joined up with some foreign girl, another chicken in the pot. This one's no use to us anymore!'

He half turned away, drew his Bowie and, spinning on his heel, drove it into Flynn's stomach, ripping as it was withdrawn. The New York gambler only had time to mutter, 'I didn't...' before his shocked eyes glazed over and he expired. The only protests at the killing were from two of the gang who had had their eyes on pieces of Flynn's clothing. 'Why didn't you strip him first, chief. Now it's all bloody.'

Scar waved them to be silent. 'Mount up an' ride! From what the late Mr Flynn said there'll be plenty of new clothing in those wagons,' and leaping into their saddles, they rode at a gallop north and then west along the Mountain Trail, sure that their quarry, a mere bunch of women, were not too far ahead.

Scar was correct in his assumption. Since Abbie and Jack Harding were insistent that the women had to be able to handle their firearms, the wagon train, starting early in the morning, had averaged less than ten miles each day before halting in mid afternoon so they had time for a full hour of rifle practice – learning speed loading, aiming, shooting at marks, and each cleaning their own gun before being inspected by either their captain or Jack.

That afternoon the ex-corporal had just completed a session on snap shooting and was busy laying out some large pieces of bark at distances of twenty-five to fifty yards to act as targets when Abbie came riding in at a gallop. She, as was her usual practice, had just been completing a ride around the campsite, checking that all was satisfactory for a distance of several hundred yards, when she saw a bunch of horsemen approaching at high speed. A glance through her father's field telescope convinced her that the newcomers' intentions were not good.

'Stand to, everyone! Load your rifles. Prepare to repel a probable attack!'

So ordering, Abbie hitched the bay inside the wagon circle, and set the example by swiftly loading her Springfield and checking the loads in her revolver. The defenders were all at their posts by the time the rough-looking riders had halted, at a signal from their leader, about fifty yards from the wagon barricade. Scar rode out ahead of his men and called out, 'Hey! This ain't no decent way to receive neighbours when they come avisiting. Put up your guns! We come in peace.'

Unfortunately, Scar's attempt at gaining an entry by guile was fruitless on two accounts. First of all, several of his own men grinned, and one actually sniggered, at his portrayal of the uncouth bunch of ruffians as being but peaceful citizens. Secondly, and more telling, was Dora's cry, which was rapidly spread among the defenders, 'He's riding White Blaze, Len Flynn's sorrel. I'd know that horse anywhere!'

71

THE PINFIRE LADY

Abbie had stepped outside of the wagon circle and was poised ready for trouble. Scar heard Dora's cry and knew that his ploy had failed. He therefore turned to his men and cried, 'OK you wolverines. Get them!'

As he gave his order, Abbie dropped to one knee and fired her rifle. She aimed at Scar, but his horse reared at the moment she pulled her trigger, and the ball struck the sorrel in the head killing him instantly. Scar jumped clear as the horse fell and ran forward, Bowie brandished in his right hand, pistol in his left. Simultaneously, Jack Harding gave the order for his front line of defence to open fire. This consisted of the six women from the newly-joined wagon train while he, his wife Polly, Jacob Levy and young Bobby Smith acted as a second line, ready to fire as the first group reloaded.

Abbie dropped her rifle and, pulling her 12mm pinfire, put two head shots into the advancing Scar. He reeled back and dropped like a stone. The fire of the women had been equally devastating. Three of the gang were down and not moving, while a fourth squirmed around on the ground, both hands clutching his stomach while he screamed for his long-dead mother. As the front rank reloaded, Jack and the other three stepped forward and, using independent fire, brought down more of the outlaws. One, and one only, rode away out of rifle range, clutching a shattered right shoulder and crying, 'Don't shoot! Please don't shoot!' as, terrified, he retreated from the murderous fire.

Jack Harding stalked forward and put a merciful ball into the gut-shot outlaw's head. Abbie saw the stern look on his face and queried, 'Jack?'

'They got Polly, the murdering bastards!'

His wife had fired as directed and, instead of stepping under cover to reload, had stood there in the open and a chance shot had hit her in the heart, killing her instantly. The only other casualty was Eve Schultz who had been hit in the left arm. The ball had missed the bones, but had made a painful furrow from wrist to elbow. She, however, assured Abbie that it was nothing to worry about.

The bodies of the renegades were dragged some distance from the trail, and laid in a row beneath a sign 'outlaws' burnt into a board. Their weapons were smashed and left in a pile, while their surviving horses, except for one that Jack Harding kept for himself, were unsaddled and turned loose. A grave was dug for the remains of Polly Harding, and the whole group gathered to pay their last respects. They had no minister or priest among them so Abbie, as leader, spoke with a lump in her throat of how Polly had been such a pleasant, willing team-mate for both Jack and the assembled group. Most of the women were quietly crying by the time Abbie ended up by reciting the Lord's Prayer, while Jacob whispered the Jewish Prayer for the Dead. Then the grave was filled in, and a simple wooden cross placed over the site, marking the spot where yet another person had died during the western expansion of the United States.

Abbie saw that something would have to be done to relieve the sombre mood that pervaded the group. So she gave the order to prepare to move out. Animals were brought in, hitched up and, seemingly, in no time all were ready to leave what became known as slaughter camp.

Abbie, seated astride her bay, looked around to ensure that all was ready. She raised her right arm on high and cried out, 'Wagons roll!'

CHAPTER NINE

Because of the changed circumstances, Jack Harding and Jacob Levy decided to team up. Jacob's cart was hitched behind Jack's wagon, which the former now drove most of the time, leaving the ex-corporal free to do some of the scouting. They shared the cooking arrangements in which Abbie also joined. Fortunately, the trio seemed to get on well together and Jacob, not being an Orthodox Jew, had no dietary problems.

The afternoon following the battle of slaughter camp, they had hardly circled the wagons when Abbie noted yet more riders approaching from the east. Their uniformity in appearance and the western sun glinting off brass buttons and accoutrements indicated that these horsemen presented no danger.

Arriving at the camp and speaking to Abbie, the leader of the cavalry patrol introduced himself, 'Lieutenant Perkins, ma'am, Fourth Cavalry. Whom do I have the honour of addressing?'

Abbie introduced herself as Penraven and indicated

that she was leader of the wagon train. Briefly, she outlined the events since leaving Paradise, ending with the defeat of the outlaw gang the previous day. In her description, Abbie gave due credit to the part played by Jack Harding and stressed that their successful defence had in large measure been due to the sturdy pioneer women.

As she spoke the lieutenant's eyes grew wider and still wider and, eventually, he burst out with, 'Well, if that don't beat the band! So that's how Scar and his bunch of scalawags met their end. Do you know Miss, er, Captain Penraven, we've been trailing those rogues for weeks, ever since they looted a lonely ranch near the settlement of Cheyenne. You folks did the army and the country a good service in getting rid of them!' and turning to Jack who was standing by he stated, 'And you, sir, if you're not tired of soldiering, we could certainly find a place for you in the Fourth Cavalry.'

Jack smiled at the invitation and shook his head. 'No, sir, thankee for the offer, but I've had me fill of soldiering. I'll stick with the captain here.'

The patrol was invited to eat and spend the night at the wagon site and, nothing loath, the cavalrymen were delighted to eat something other than army rations. It was a delightful evening. The men dined on home cooking, and the women feasted their eyes on the men and enjoyed having male company, if only for one evening. Abbie tended to keep herself aloof from the merriment. Not because she considered herself in any way superior to the other women but, being in command, she recalled her father's oft-repeated comments that too much familiarity would invariably loosen discipline to the detriment of any

76

unit. So she sat, a lonely figure, by the side of Jack's wagon, industriously stripping and cleaning her pinfire pistol, and tried to ignore the happy laughter coming from the camp-fires. The cavalrymen looked over and watched her as, pistol gleaming, she practised drawing and snapping her pistol on an empty chamber as she did every evening. The whole group watched in awe at her fluid pistol play and Jacob whispered, 'No vonder men call 'er The Pinfire Lady!'

And thus, when the patrol left the following morning, Abbie's reputation as a pistolera left with them.

The days and weeks passed. Like all the other parties moving westward, whether isolated groups, small caravans like themselves, or huge trains with up to seventy-five or more wagons, in general, they all experienced similar situations. Water had to be found, both for stock and human consumption. Rivers had to be crossed and Abbie was thankful that her people did not have to break down banks to afford passage for their wagons. Earlier trains had performed this task for them.

There were days for all travellers when the relentless wind, coming out of the west, drove both people and animals crazy with frustration as, with bleary, red-rimmed, grit-filled eyes, they drove their reluctant oxen and horses forward. Inevitably, every wagon train had sickness created by many diverse causes. Some camps were insanitary, when foolish travellers took water downstream from where they watered their stock or where others earlier had performed their ablutions. For some, the dietary limitations and lack of green vegetables took their toll among the thousands

77

travelling west, and their graves along the trails marked the unanticipated end of their individual journeys. There were locations where the dreaded cholera or smallpox broke out and, due to limited medical knowledge, would spread like wildfire through an encampment. Babies were born, and babies died, as did the mothers that had borne them, and their final resting places, with a wooden cross or merely some pieces of stone to prevent wild animals digging up the bodies, were solitary reminders to all that passed by that life was a fragile thing.

In addition to all of the foregoing, the pioneers had to contend with wolves, four-legged creatures that tried to seize their stock, and two-legged varieties that preyed upon both people and their animals. The Plains Indians resented these 'white eyes' from the east, who came in their lumbering wagons, killing the buffalo and other wild game, in many cases not because they were hungry, but just because they could. They desecrated sacred burial sites, wantonly cut down the forests to build more and more permanent dwellings for themselves and their kin, and then told the native tribes that this was their land. They had found it!

The problem was that both cultures had totally different notions about private property and land ownership, and, of course, both were certain that they were right. The result was that there was was intermittent warfare where wagon trains were attacked and, on occasion, wiped out, with both animals and people slaughtered and their contents looted. In return, settlers would assemble armed force and attack and destroy Indian villages, without attempting to determine whether they were guilty of hostility towards the Whites. 'The only good Indian is a dead Indian' was a common saying of the day.

There were also the gangs of renegade Whites and half-breeds of all colours who, like the pirates who were the scourge of the Mississippi River, attempted to rob, steal and kill travellers on the trails to the West. Abbie and her people were lucky that they did not encounter any of this breed, but from others they heard some hair-raising accounts that kept them continually on their guard. They did, however, have one meeting with Indians, which could easily have become a serious affair.

One morning while the wagons were still circled, young Bobby Smith, on guard duty, yelled out that Indians were coming. Quickly, everyone was at her or his place, rifles loaded, ready to repel any attack. The Indians drew near and Abbie, who had stepped out of the circle, was relieved to note that they were not wearing war paint. She raised her hand in the peace sign.

The leader rode forward, 'Squaw give guns! Give whiskey!'

Abbie shook her head firmly. 'No guns, Chief, also no whiskey! You can have some bacon and a sack of flour. That's all we can spare our red brothers!' She signalled, and Tom brought out the offerings and placed them on the ground.

The chief reiterated his demands for whiskey and guns and then frowned, 'Where white chief? No talk to squaw!' he declared disdainfully.

'I am the chief here. You talk to me!'

He looked down in surprise and grinned, noticing Abbie's pistol hanging prominently in its cross side draw.

'Show Red Hawk how squaw shoot man's gun!'

Using a mixture of words and sign language, Abbie had one of the braves take the Chief's gaily painted shield and place it against a rock about ten yards away. She turned back toward the chief and then swinging round, drew and rapidly poured five bullets into the centre of the shield. Then, while Red Hawk still sat mouth open in wonder, she punched out her empty shell cases and reloaded swiftly, trying to appear very casual.

Red Hawk exclaimed, 'Wah!' (which Jack Harding later suggested was an Indian variation of 'Blimey!') and proceeded to speak to his men, raising his arm, bringing it down in a jagged gesture, and pointing to Abbie, 'Squaw Chief, sister to lightning! We go in peace.'

And so saying, the side of bacon and the flour were picked up and they rode away. The word spread far and wide and, in the future, all the Indian tribes knew Abbie as 'Sister Lightning.'

CHAPTER TEN

For some time the travellers had periodically caught glimpses of the Arkansas River to their south as they headed west. They passed through about sixty miles of wooded country known, for its majestic trees, as Big Timbers. While it was delightful to travel in partial shade, escaping the constant glare of the sun, it was also a time demanding full alertness as there were many places where a caravan could be ambushed.

Eventually Big Timbers was left behind and the next landmark Abbie was to watch for was Bent's New Fort.

William Bent and his brother Charles, together with their partner Colonel St Vrain, had in the 1830s built a large adobe fort, not too far from the town of La Punta. Trading with the Indian tribes, the mountain men and the caravans heading to and from Santa Fe, the Bents and St Vrain had, for several years, a flourishing trade in furs, hides and other products. By 1849 the beaver trade was dead, however, and William Bent attempted to sell his fort to the US Army. They declined to buy the fort and so, using twenty covered wagons, Bent emptied the buildings of everything movable and blew the structure up. He and his employees built another adobe fort, about fifty miles east of their former location, and this was the landmark that Abbie sought.

The fort hove in sight and, as they drew nearer, seemed to be an impressive building, though by all accounts, only half as big as the one that had been destroyed. They drew up in an area obviously used by caravans and, for the first time in many weeks, did not circle their wagons. Jack arranged for two others apart from himself to remain in camp, and the remainder went to patronise the trading store in the fort, while Abbie went to pay her respects to William Bent.

She found him, a cheery, round-faced, middle-aged man, in his quarters and his weather-beaten features broke into a broad smile when she entered and introduced herself.

'Aha! So, you're the Pinfire Lady I've been hearing about. I'm pleased to make your acquaintance, ma'am. We've sure heard a lot about you!'

'Thank you Mr Bent, but just call me Penraven, or better still, Abbie.'

Abbie was seated and, with a soft drink in hand, was soon at ease and persuaded to relate most of her story to William Bent and his Cheyenne wife Owl Woman. There were certain things that Abbie kept to herself, and others, such as the search for her missing investment property, that she stressed were not to be voiced abroad.

When her story was finished, Abbie rose to leave and was

encouraged to stay a while and enjoy supper with her hospitable host and hostess. The hour was quite late when she finally arose and, after thanking her hosts, Abbie made her way along the darkened porch that fronted the interior of the fort. Suddenly, she was aware of a dark shadow looming up in front of her and, by the dim light of a solitary hanging lantern, she beheld a huge, scruffy, bearded man in her path, reeking with the alcohol he had consumed, and maintaining his balance by swaying to and fro.

'Where you goin', lil girl? Les' you an' me find a nice place where we can make love. Come on!'

So saying, he made a swift grab with his left hand, and grabbed Abbie by the front of her shirt. Ignoring her struggles, he jerked her towards him at the same time as he swept his right arm around her, locking her rigidly against his shirt reeking with sour sweat. Abbie struggled in vain against his drunken advances, as he fought to turn her face towards his, vainly trying to plant a kiss on her.

'Let go of me, you drunken fool!' Abbie cried, as her attacker transferred his left hand to her breast, pawing savagely, squeezing and twisting. Abbie cried out with the pain and wriggled frantically.

Suddenly, she received a slap across the face that set her head singing. 'Shut up, you slut! Jus' behave, an' accept your lot.' And he started to drag her towards a darkened doorway.

Abbie resisted wildly. Her left arm was trapped against his body, as was her pinfire pistol. With a supreme effort, she got her right hand beneath her buckskin shirt and against the hideout Colt. Drawing the gun, yet unable to raise it, she fired at the only possible target, down at her assailant's crotch. Her would-be rapist screamed in anguish, as Abbie fired again and yet again. He held both hands to his mangled manhood and stared at her, his face twisted with pain.

'You stinkin' bitch! I'm gonna kill you for this!'

Abbie stood aghast at the havoc caused by his advances. Now, she had to react immediately, as a glistening Bowie appeared in his blood-stained hand and swept in her direction. Dropping the Colt, she stepped back and, drawing her 12mm pinfire, she put two bullets into his head between the close-set eyes. The bear-like figure remained still for a split second before swaying and crashing to the floor.

Abbie stood leaning against one of the porch pillars, smoking pistol in hand, as she was surrounded by excited people, drawn to the scene of the assault by the sound of the shots. Mr and Mrs Bent pushed their way through the crowd and, reaching her side, William queried, 'What exactly happened here, Abbie?'

Still attempting to regain her composure, Abbie, in short, panting sentences, described the attack and her reaction. There were muttered noises of approval from the crowd of men as, in the West, most women were considered to be off-limits to male advances – unless they were 'sporting girls' and, even then, one was supposed to approach with a certain amount of decorum. Rape, or attempts at same, was simply beyond the Pale and, in most cases, the transgressor received little or no sympathy.

A lantern was produced and William Bent peered down at the bloody corpse. 'Why it's Pierre LaRue! He was most certainly a bad 'un, thoroughly evil. Problem is, he has a twin brother, Paul, as debonair as this one was uncouth, and just as evil, or possibly far more so. He has the reputation of being a fast gun and, when he gets the news of Pierre's death, he's going to come running to avenge his twin. I think perhaps you'd better pull out in the early morning.'

Abbie shook her head. 'No, Mr Bent! Thank you for the advice, and I'm sorry that in a way, I'm the one who has brought this calamity down upon you. No, I cannot run away. My people need rest, and if I run, then I'm sure Mr LaRue is bound to follow, and probably catch me on the trail. No, with your permission we'll stay here, and if trouble comes, I'll try to keep it outside of the fort!'

A bystander retrieved Abbie's Colt and handed it to her. Jack Harding arrived and insisted on escorting his captain back to the wagon encampment. Thanking the Bents once more and promising to see them in the morning, Abbie was glad to be away from the gawking crowd that was always attracted by the excitement of any gunplay.

They walked silently. Abbie was lost in her own thoughts and Jack respected her need for privacy. Arriving at their wagons, she sat down by the fire shivering and buried her face in her hands.

'Why me?' she thought. 'I had no desire to obtain the awful reputation that I seem to have acquired! People are looking upon me as a killer and I'm not.' She thought back, 'Jake and the Mexican? I had no choice. It was them or me – the same with Cad Williams and Scar. In each case, they were the ones who initiated the shooting. I was merely defending myself and my people.'

Abbie's sad reverie was interrupted by Jacob Levy who

thrust a hot cup of steaming liquid into her hands, ' 'Ere dearie, 'ave a nice 'ot cuppa tea. Me old mum always said in time of trouble there was nuffink better to cheer a soul up. That's right, drink it 'ot!'

Gradually the tea took effect and the shivering ceased. Abbie considered her options. She could leave, cease the quest for the property that her father appeared to have held in this part of the world, resume her former name and title, travel by stage to Santa Fe and thence back to the East Coast. What then? Back to England to her late husband's ruined estate or, worse still, back to a life with Aunt Sarah? Abbie shuddered at the thought. 'Yes, Aunt Sarah! No, Aunt Sarah!' and to sit there decorously while listening to inane conversations? 'No! Such a life would not be living!' She would take her chances here in the West and, as the locals would state, 'let the chips fall where they may!'

In the morning Abbie called her people together for a frank discussion. All had heard details of the previous night's shooting, and everyone was curious about the purpose of the meeting. Rather than dwelling upon that incident, Abbie stated that it was still her intention to travel north to the Pike's Peak area, probably to the community known as Colorado City. Did they still want to continue to travel with her, or would they prefer to make other arrangements?

There was an immediate chorus of voices all stating that they wanted to remain united as one party and Abbie felt gratified by their response.

'In that case,' she said, 'Perhaps we should at this time

consider what, in a general sort of way, are our individual plans at the end of our journey?'

Jacob shrugged his thin shoulders and indicated that, as they all well knew, he wanted to start peddling his wares when they reached the end of trail. Until that time, he was willing to assist any of his fellow travellers in need of assistance.

The women looked at each other waiting for someone to begin. Finally, Nelly Smith looked at her son Tom, he nodded and she stated that their plans were that he would find work in one of the mines while she figured on taking in washing, noting that with all of the menfolk there she should have no lack of business.

Ann Marlowe and Beth Isaacson had obviously discussed this topic for some time, and they stated that they intended to pool their resources and open an eating place, nothing fancy, just a place where hungry miners could get a good hot meal.

Naomi Johnson and Eve Schultz were a trifle more ambitious. They said that they believed it would not be too long before there were more womenfolk in the area, and so they intended to stock up with bolts of cloth, lace and reels of cotton from Bent's Store and open a ladies' dress shop. Then they all turned and looked expectantly at Dora McAdam.

She blushed, looked down at her feet, smiled and said sweetly, 'Well, I guess it all depends what Mr Harding is doing!' And there was general laughter as that worthy hid his face in his coat.

He emerged and said, 'Well, I'm sticking with the captain as long as she needs me. So I guess Dora's plans will have to fit in with mine.'

Thus, there was complete agreement that they would continue together as a united wagon train and, with that in mind, all set to refurbish their wagons and harness and check stores for the next long haul.

CHAPTER ELEVEN

Days later, many miles to the south-west in Santa Fe, a black-haired, dark, sinister-looking man, clothed in the style of a Mississippi gambler, was having a series of losing hands at the poker table in the Golden Nugget saloon. His temper, always short even under the most pleasurable circumstances, was close to bursting into some violent action, seeing his money going in a constant flow to the other side of the table with each and every hand.

A man hurried in and whispered loudly to him, 'Pierre's been shot by some woman up at Bent's Fort! The news has only just reached here!'

Momentarily stunned by the news, the gambler sat frozen, his cards clutched in his hands. The teamster across the table then made the mistake of his life. 'Come on, let's get on with the game! Your turn! Forget about this goddamn Pierre, whoever he is – or was, rather!'

He sniggered at his little joke. It was the last thing he ever spoke. Paul LaRue exploded! Flinging the cards down, he called his poker opponent a series of vile epithets, describing his ancestry in no uncertain terms.

Finally, the man was stung into action and started to draw his pistol. LaRue let him clear leather, and then swiftly drew a Navy Colt from a shoulder holster and shot the teamster dead. Turning to the onlookers he observed, 'You see! He drew first. I fired in self defence!'

None of the bystanders disputed his version of the argument and its outcome. Paul LaRue was a dangerous man at the best of times; in this mood, it was like sitting next to a keg of gunpowder ready to explode at any second.

He got up and went outside, lighting a thin cigar and, leaning against the porch rail, thought furiously to himself, 'Damn, Pierre! You may have been my twin brother, but were never *mon ami*. Still, now I must go and avenge your miserable death, because it is expected of me. Failure to do so will lessen my standing here in Santa Fe. "Oh, LaRue, he's not that great! He's actually allowed a woman to frighten him!" '

He paced slowly up and down the porch, drawing furiously upon his cigar, and swiftly came to the conclusion that he had no other choice. He must drop all his plans in Santa Fe and ride north to Bent's Fort, find this unknown woman, dispose of her and return. 'Who was she?' he wondered. 'Probably some dance hall trash that Pierre picked up somewhere and shot him over non-payment for services rendered.'

His cigar was thrown into the street and, returning to his rented room, he packed a bag and made his way to the livery stable where his horse was kept. The ostler resented being awakened at the late hour but, sensing the foul mood exhibited by Paul LaRue, he hurried to do his bidding. His horse saddled and a pack horse rented,

90

LaRue's next stop was a General Store where he pounded on the door until an irate, but cautious, storekeeper grudgingly allowed the gambler entry, and sold him extra fine powder and percussion caps for his .36 calibre Colt Navy revolvers and a grubstake for his journey. Equipped and armed, Paul LaRue mounted his horse and, leading his pack animal, headed north up the Mountain Branch trail towards Bent's Fort.

Meanwhile, at the wagon encampment outside Bent's Fort, Abbie and her party spent some time repairing equipment and clothing and stocking up on foodstuffs and other items which would not be available on the trail north.

Abbie paid a special visit to William Bent. 'Mr Bent, perhaps you can assist me.'

Bent looked up from the ledger over which he was poring and smiled, 'Why certainly, Abbie. If it's in my power, I'll be only too pleased to assist you. What's the problem?'

Abbie produced a 12mm cartridge and handed it to him. 'Would you be able to order more of these?'

She explained that the ones she had were apparently British-made, although her pistol was of a French design. She tried to conserve her use of the ammunition but, inevitably, her stock was going to diminish and she would have to replace them.

William Bent nodded and reaching up pulled down a large catalogue inscribed 'Schuyler, Hartley and Graham, Sporting Goods'.

'Let's see what these fellas have to offer.' He thumbed through the book with a practised hand and, finding the

91

section on fixed ammunition, declared, 'Genuine pinfire cartridges, available in many calibres. Hmm, nine, eleven, twelve and fifteen mm. How many do you want me to order?'

Abbie thought for a moment and then suggested, 'Five hundred, please. I know that seems like a lot, but I don't know how many I'll need, nor when I can re-order. Would that be in order?'

'Certainly, dear lady! I'll hold them when they get here until I get a forwarding address. You can pay me at that time.'

Abbie insisted that she wanted to pay in advance as, if affairs went badly for her, she might not be around to settle her debts. After a little hesitation, she produced a Letter of Credit drawn upon an English bank and handed it to William Bent.

He looked at it and his eyes opened wide, 'Lady Penraven! You mean to tell me that you. . . .' He stopped in confusion, as Abbie held up her hand.

'Yes, I'm the widow of Lord Penraven, but I would rather that does not become common knowledge.'

And Abbie elaborated on the details of her North American journey and misadventures. She described how she was intending to find out what had happened to her father's investment, and thought it better to remain incognito for the time being. Meanwhile, if perhaps Mr Bent could possibly advance some money against the Letter of Credit, it would be appreciated. The matter was soon settled and Abbie walked back to her encampment with a comfortable wad of American bills in her possession. William Bent signalled to one of his trusted

Mexican employees. 'Miguel! That lady who just left, she has a very bad enemy, and I'm sure that he'll come looking for her.'

'*Sí, Señor*! You mean the gambling man who is brother to the one that La Pinfire Señorita had to kill. I know him. What you want me to do?'

'Just keep your eyes open and, if you see him, let me know and warn the lady that trouble has arrived at the fort.'

Miguel happily accepted his role as lookout for the lovely señorita and left to go about his everyday tasks.

As the other members of her wagon train went about the work of getting ready for the next stage of their journey, Abbie, in addition to keeping a general eye on every aspect of things that concerned her people, had resumed an earlier exercise. Every day, but at varying times, she would saddle up her bay and ride out to a little hidden arroyo she had discovered, and there she would diligently spend the best part of an hour practising drawing and dry-firing her pinfire revolver. Due to her need to conserve her ammunition, her amount of live fire had to be limited to one or two shots per day using, as she had in Billy's cabin, the 'chimney piece' to ensure that her accuracy had not diminished.

Jack Harding was worried about her heading out alone every day, and argued that he should accompany her, but Abbie was insistent that she went alone. Being well armed, and constantly checking her surroundings, Abbie felt confident that she was not in danger, unaware that peril was getting closer with every hoof-beat on the mountain trail.

*

Finally one mid-morning Paul LaRue arrived at Bent's
Fort. Miguel saw him riding in, dressed in his habitual suit
of black broadcloth, white frilled shirt and black cravat
with a low-crowned black hat low on his forehead and ran
to tell William Bent that the 'avenging one' had come.
Over the years Bent had dealt with hundreds of men,
some good and some bad. Paul LaRue was one of the
latter. Nevertheless, he strolled out and greeted him, 'Paul
LaRue, to what do we owe this pleasure? Get down and
come and have a cooling drink.'

LaRue dismounted, 'Howdy Bent! Don't tell me that
you're glad to see me. What happened to Pierre?'

William Bent was equally blunt with his explanation,
'Your brother got drunk and went on a rampage. He
assaulted a woman with intent to rape her. She resisted violently. He pulled that Bowie of his and attacked her. So,
she shot him dead!'

After a moments silence, he added, 'I had Pierre buried
in the little cemetery up on the bluff. We had a clergyman
passing through. He read the burial service over him. His
knife and other stuff is in the storeroom.'

Paul LaRue muttered his thanks, but seemed lost in
thought. 'This woman, where did he pick her up?'

'I'm telling you, Paul. This lady had just had supper
with me and Owl Woman, and was heading back to her
own camp when Pierre attacked her. He was the guilty
party.'

The gambler shrugged his shoulders and indicated that
it made no difference. Pierre had to be avenged. Failure to
take action would reflect back on him, as he would be considered indecisive. Besides which, there was a blood debt

94

outstanding and it had to be paid.

'Send somebody to find this woman and inform her that I wish to seek satisfaction! I will be on the bluff, by the cemetery, at three o'clock this afternoon. Now, I will have that drink, and perhaps will buy a luncheon. Maybe I can find someone to have a little game of cards with to pass away the time?'

Shaking his head, Bent sent Miguel off to inform Abbie of the challenge. He wished that there was more he could do, but the Code of the West at that time was rigid. If a challenge was presented, it had to be answered. True, he'd never imagined one involving a woman, but it certainly was not impossible.

Miguel reached the wagon encampment and delivered the message to Abbie who was speaking to Jack Harding at the time. Jack reacted violently, protesting that his wagon captain should not even respond to the challenge. Abbie shook her head and motioned Jack to be quiet, 'Tell Mr LaRue that I am quite prepared to meet his challenge! Jack, perhaps you would consider being my second in this affair?'

Muttering audibly, Jack grudgingly agreed, and so the strange duel was arranged. Jack insisted that their positions should be located so that neither would have the advantage of the afternoon sun, and LaRue sent a note that this was acceptable.

Abbie had considered her situation very seriously. Through no fault of her own, she had been forced to end the life of Pierre LaRue, and then along comes his twin brother, a publicly acclaimed gunfighter, determined to obtain retribution for his brother's death. She realized that if the duel did not take place now, there would be other occasions in the future where Paul LaRue might appear, still seeking vengeance.

What did she know about her adversary? Abbie knew that he originally hailed from New Orleans. He made his living from gambling at the card tables, therefore, he must be confident, shrewd and calculating. He habitually carried two .36 calibre Navy Colts, one in a belt holster on the left hip, the other in a shoulder holster, again on the left side. His approach in a gunfight, apparently, was to give his opponent the impression that his right hand was dropping to draw his belt-gun, but to move the shorter distance and pull the concealed one instead. Abbie realized that Paul LaRue represented the toughest fighter she had yet to face. How could she possibly win against such an opponent? As Billy would have said, she needed an edge.

The time drew close to the appointed hour. Abbie sat by Jack's wagon, carefully polishing her pistol and each shell case before reloading and slipping the weapon up and down in her holster several times to ensure that it would clear when needed. She had considered dressing more elaborately, but eventually just remained in her old trail garb of slouch hat and buckskin shirt and pants. Looking out towards the bluff, she saw that a figure, undoubtedly Paul LaRue, was walking steadily to the designated location. Abbie decided to let him stand in the hot sun a little while before she too arose leisurely, and slowly strolled up to where he was waiting.

'You're late!' snapped LaRue to the handsome-looking woman walking towards him, her feminine hips swaying provocatively with every step.

'*Bonjour*, Monsieur LaRue! Surely, as a gentleman, you know that it is a woman's prerogative to be late, especially when she goes to meet a man?' Abbie's remarks were all in French, painfully learned from her tutor, Mr Williams, in India, during her tender years.

Paul LaRue was startled to be addressed in the tongue of his childhood, and especially to be reminded of the code of manners expected of a gentleman. He pulled himself together and spat out harshly, 'Talk English, damn you! You killed my brother and I'm going to give you the same treatment!'

Abbie goaded him, further referring to Pierre as a filthy *cochon*, who had not deserved to live!

She watched Paul's eyes and noted that his well-reputed temper was close to boiling point. Suddenly, his right hand darted sideways. As he made his move, Abbie took a step to the left, dropped to one knee, drew her pinfire revolver and fired, holding the gun steady in the two-handed grip. Her aim was true. LaRue's Colt had hardly cleared leather when Abbie's first shot smashed into his chest, and a second hit almost in the same place. Despite receiving two mortal wounds, his hand moved instinctively to raise his pistol. The gun was at no more than forty-five degrees when his thumb slipped off the hammer spur, and he fired just one shot that thudded into the ground at Abbie's feet. Paul LaRue dropped his Colt and stood there swaying, a bewildered look on his swarthy features, and then, without a sound, he fell forward on his face.

Abbie heard a distant cheer and turning saw Jack, Dora and several others of the wagon train, as well as Mr and Mrs Bent and a number of their retainers ascending the hill. She was still standing there frozen, her pistol still in her hand when they arrived and surrounded her, 'Well done, Captain!' declared Jack Harding, 'We was all hoping an' praying that you would pull it off. It's a bloomin' miracle, that's what it is!'

William Bent was far more subdued than Abbie's second-in-command, but in his own way equally effusive. 'Abbie, don't worry yourself about the death of this wretch! He was a thoroughly evil man, and the world is a far better place with him out of the way. We will bury him next to his brother Pierre and that will be the end of the matter.'

CHAPTER TWELVE

The wagon train left the next day. Farewells had been said, stores loaded and augmented by an additional five vehicles whose owners had approached Abbie seeking permission to travel with her. The wagons rolled west. Abbie had demanded of the newcomers the same stipulation as with her original group. They must possess firearms and demonstrate an ability and willingness to use them. She would carry no passengers.

All were bound for the area around Pike's Peak where, it was said, gold could be picked up by the handful from the ground and in the many streams. There was a constant stream of people in wagons, various types of other conveyances, and even lone travellers on foot, all hurrying towards this fabled Eldorado. If they were wise, people journeyed together in groups such as Abbie's. There was comfort in moving together: safety in numbers, security in the event of accidents, more chance of assistance if sickness occurred and a general feeling that one was not alone in this strange and dangerous land.

Night after night, Abbie had spent some considerable

time going over her father's papers, concerning the property that he was understood to have left to his daughter. There was a horse ranch and considerable acreage in the vicinity of a community described as Colorado City, although Abbie had come to realize that, in North America, a city might well be but a dozen houses, with possibly a general store and probably a saloon. Several town lots were registered in the name of Major Frederick Martin, her father, as was the deed to a mining venture, described as being two miles north-east of the eminence known as Pike's Peak.

Back in England, Abbie had left all business dealings to Bertie Penraven, her late unlamented husband. She recalled the discussions that they had and, in retrospect, thought it a little strange that Bertie had made no reference to anything other than the gold mine.

Prior to her departure from Bent's Fort, she had a long discussion with William Bent and had showed him the papers. The agent in charge of Major Martin's affairs in this part of the world had been a George Gillis. Included with the deeds was a brief letter stating that Mr Gillis had met with a fatal accident and that a certain Roger Fenton was handling the accounts. Attached had been a mining dividend, in United States dollars, payable to Frederick Martin or bearer. After that communication there had been silence.

Bent had suggested that the first thing she should do upon arriving in the region was to find a reputable lawyer and lay the case before him, meanwhile remaining quiet about her identity either as Major Martin's heir or as Lady Penraven. In the case of the latter, there should not be too much trouble as there were many Cornishmen in the mines, and Penraven was a common Cornish surname. He gave her a note of introduction to a young lawyer, Daniel Clifford, whom he understood to have hung out his shingle in Colorado City.

'I know him and I've had dealings with him. I'm sure that he'll respect your confidences and do the square thing for you.'

Abbie had tucked the note in with the other papers and, having stowed the documents away, resolved to put the matter out of her mind and just concentrate on her wagon train and the trail.

Her information indicated that they should be heading for Fountain Creek, a growing settlement which, Abbie was told, looked as though it was here to stay, unlike so many others whose empty, roofless shacks and gaping doorways were mute testimony to abandoned ambitions. From Fountain Creek, a trail ran north on the east side of Boiling Creek. Where that trail split, with the right fork heading up to Russellville and Montana City, bearing left would take a traveller to Colorado City a few miles north-west.

A week's uneventful journeying found them at the out-skirts of Fountain Creek. The wagons were circled and Abbie, accompanied by Jack, rode into the settlement seeking information regarding the condition of the northern trail.

Fountain Creek displayed the usual straggling array of shacks, some with sod roofs and others with cedar shakes, along with two or three more pretentious false-fronted buildings with a boardwalk and hitching rail. One announced to the world that it was a General Store and so, dismounting, they both entered and enquired of the grey-haired lady at the counter whether she had any information to offer about the state of the trail heading towards Pike's Peak.

'I'm sorry, I can't help you folks. I've never gone up that far an' my man is lyin' sick wi' the fever. I daren't disturb him.' She looked quite crestfallen at her inability to assist them and then her face brightened, 'Tell you what, though! Henry Stickler goes up that way regular. He's jus' bin in here an' was goin' next door fer a drink. Ask Henry an' he'll tell ye's what you need ter know.'

They thanked her and left. At the batwing doors of the saloon Abbie paused, and indicated that Jack should go in and ask, since it was not customary for ladies to enter drinking establishments, unless they were of the sporting variety. Jack went in, while Abbie waited patiently outside, ignoring the curious glances of the odd passer-by. Suddenly there was a loud crash from within the saloon followed by a medley of voices with some raised in anger. Peering over the batwings, Abbie beheld Jack being held firmly by two large men, while a third even larger brute held him by his shirt front and prepared to smash his over-sized fist into his victim's face.

Abbie was just preparing to lethally intervene when an authoritative voice ordered, 'That's enough of that in here. If you boys want to have a bit of a dust up get outside. I don't want this place busted up.'

She looked closer into the gloomy interior and saw an elegantly dressed man waving a six-shooter to emphasize that he meant what he said.

'Furthermore, let's have one against one, shall we?'

Reluctantly, the trio released their grips on Jack, who straightened his attire and indicated that he was quite prepared to fight them one at a time. The Goliath-sized bully grinned with a wicked leer and said, 'All right, let's get outside an' see whatcha made of!' and they, followed by most of the patrons, swarmed out of the saloon and stepped into the street. Abbie was concerned, although somewhat impressed that Jack, in passing, gave her a huge wink.

The dandy was just preparing to lay down some basic rules when Goliath, head down, rushed at Jack who stepped aside to avoid his opponent's onslaught and, at the right moment, brought his clasped hands down with tremendous force on the back of the giant neck. That blow, and his own impetus, caused Jack's adversary to stumble forward where he crashed headfirst into the oak side of the horse trough and lay there stunned.

'All right, you blighters, who else wants ter 'ave a go?'

Jack stood there poised like a modern day Tom Cribb prepared to take on all comers. Nobody rushed forward to take up Jack's challenge. In fact most of the crowd looked down at their feet, shuffled them, and moved back, leaving Jack in a widened circle.

Finally, one of the pair who had held Jack in the saloon indicated that he'd accept the challenge and slipped off his coat, folded it, and walked to put it on the seat of a waiting wagon. Suddenly he turned, and uncurled a twenty-foot bullwhip.

'Now, stranger, you're about to get a first class lesson from a bullwhacker on how to use a whip!' So saying, he flicked the whip underhand and removed a small piece of Jack's left ear.

Abbie knew of the awful destruction that could be done by an expert using a bullwhip. So as he raised his whip poised to strike again, she drew and fired, her bullet smashing into the bullwhacker's wrist causing his weapon to drop from nerveless fingers.

There was stunned silence from the crowd. The bull-whacker stood, left hand clutching his shattered one. The third of the unsavoury trio cried out, 'Who fired that shot?' and noticing Abbie standing there with smoking pistol demanded. 'Who do you think are to interfere wi' two men fighting?'

The deadly accuracy of Abbie's one shot momentarily escaped him. All he saw was a small female holding a gun, a man's weapon, and butting in on an affair which to him was none of her business.

'Who I am, fellow, is none of your business! But people along the Santa Fe Trail have nicknamed me the Pinfire Lady, and that man there, whom your confederate was about to maim or even possibly blind, is my second in command! Do I make myself perfectly clear?' And, raising the pinfire, she shot his hat from his head.

The elegantly dressed man who had ordered the fight to be switched from the saloon to the street stepped out of the crowd. 'You men had no intention of having a fair fight. I suggest that you all clear out of town immediately. And don't come back!'

This advice was echoed by most of the crowd who then started drifting back into the saloon. The dandified gen-tleman approached Abbie and lifted his hat, 'Richard

104

Wootton, at your service, ma'am, commonly known in these parts as 'Uncle Dick'. Would you permit me to escort you to the dining portion of the saloon? I would be delighted to have both you and your companion as my guests.'

Abbie looked at Jack who shrugged his shoulders. 'Very well, Mr Wootton! We will be delighted to dine with you. However, we can't stay too long as we have a wagon train to attend to.'

Wootton took them through the saloon to a small area partitioned off from the main bar by a low railing. There were four small tables, only one of which was occupied. Abbie suspected from the layout that the area was more used to seeing cards, rather than food, on the tables.

They were seated and a small Mexican waiter produced a surprisingly appetizing meal when ordered, along with a bottle of French imported wine. As their meal progressed, Dick Wootton told them more about himself. A Virginian, he had left home at an early age and worked first of all as a teamster on the Santa Fe, and then as a trapper out of Bent's original fort. In fact he claimed William Bent as one of his best friends. Eventually, he had married and settled down in Taos, New Mexico, but recently had once more got the itch to travel, and was considering heading north either to Colorado City or even further to Auraria which, he suspected, was rapidly becoming a boom town. (In this he was correct. Auraria, soon to change its name to Denver, would far outstrip the surrounding communities when it came to growth.)

Abbie dug into her pouch and produced William Bent's note of introduction. Dick Wootton studied it for a moment and handed it back. 'Well, Miss Abbie, if I can assist you in any way you just tell me!'

Heartened by his warm, friendly manner, Abbie gave him a brief outline of her adventures to date and, in doing so, introduced Jack Harding into the conversation. When she described her experiences with Billy Curtis, Dick Wootton burst out laughing, 'Well I never! So you were holed up for a winter with that old mountain wolf, and he was your teacher. I've known Billy for years, and you won't find a better man this side of the Mississippi! Did he teach you the "Border roll"?'

Abbie nodded, smiling. Uncle Dick winked and, putting a forefinger to the side of his nose, nodded his head slowly. 'Old Billy has had a long varied career and many say that in his youth he rode the hoot owl trail, but that's neither here nor there. Billy's solid gold through and through and, if he taught you, no wonder you're good with that there pinfire.'

Dick Wootton paused to sip his wine and then remarked, 'Now, I understand that you folks are heading north up to the Pike's Peak area – to Colorado City to be exact. Is that correct?'

Both Abbie and Jack nodded in response to his query, and the former wondered where this conversation was leading.

'A few miles south-west of here is encamped a large wagon train, heading east to Kansas City. I've got two wagons in that caravan, with all my possessions. I and my men intended to leave the main wagon train here at Fountain Creek and go north by ourselves. However, I'd sure appreciate it if we could join up with you folks.

There's more safety in numbers and I hear that some of the tribes are pretty restless between here and your destination. What d'you say?'

Jack and Abbie remained silent, looking at each other and Dick Wootton hastened to add, 'Abbie, it'll still be your wagon train. You'll be captain as before. I'll only give you my two cents worth if I believe you may be making a wrong decision.'

After a long pause, during which time Abbie considered all the implications of adding still more people to her contingent, she thrust out her hand and said, 'Very well Uncle Dick. It's a deal. We certainly welcome having the extra firepower. Just one condition though. Your folk will have to obey my instructions as though they come from you, agreed?'

They shook hands and the deal was cemented.

CHAPTER THIRTEEN

Two days later Abbie's wagon train, joined by Dick Wootton's vehicles, headed north. The first two or three days were uneventful although, since this trail was used far less than the Santa Fe, or even the Mountain Branch, there were more obstacles to overcome. Boulders had rolled down the mountain sides since the last travellers had passed that way, and each rock, both large and small, had to be rolled out of the way before the wagons could proceed. The same was true of branches and even of small conifers of different varieties brought down by the violent storms to which the area was subject.

Abbie, sometimes alone, but frequently accompanied by either Jack or Dick Wootton, would scout ahead each day, noting the terrain and any obstacles to be overcome. Dick was with her one mid morning when she spotted smoke rising from a distant hilltop. Then there was a second thin column rising in puffs from a high bluff off to the east but ahead of them.

'Mr Wootton, do you see those smoke signals! What

does it mean? Should we perhaps warn the people and prepare for trouble?'

Dick Wootton reined in his horse, 'I've seem 'em, Abbie, just before you made your comments! Let's just wait here a moment and try to figure out what they're up to.'

Abbie got out her father's field telescope and peered at a pair of figures half hidden ahead amid a clump of young pines. 'What do you make of those, Mr Wootton?'

She handed him the 'scope, which he quickly adjusted to his focal length, and he studied the trees Abbie indicated.

One of the distant figures had stepped forward to obtain a better view of the two riders approaching and Dick Wootton gave a half stifled gasp and then said tersely, 'Young lady, we have a problem! At first I thought that we were encountering Utes, with whom I've had dealings for years. But those aren't Utes; they're Comanche who are far north of their regular territory!'

'Are they hostile, Mr Wootton?' enquired Abbie, putting a note of determination into her voice.

'They're more than hostile! They're the meanest warriors you'll meet on the plains. And why this bunch are so far north I've no idea. Now, Abbie! When I give the word, turn that bay around and ride straight for the wagon train. Fire three shots in the air as you ride, and, hopefully, Jack Harding will have got the people circled by the time we get there. Ready? Go!'

Abbie swung her bay around and spurred the horse into a gallop, while Dick Wootton did the same on his pinto. Drawing her pinfire as she rode, Abbie thumbed back the hammer and triggered a shot into the air, followed by two more. Behind them were a series of hideous bloodcurdling yells of frustration and, Abbie, risking a glance behind her, saw twenty or more war-painted Indians burst from the trees and gallop in hot pursuit after the two fleeing 'white eyes'.

She reloaded as she rode, which was just as well since ahead of them they saw two of the hostiles sliding their mounts down the steep side of a sandstone bluff with the intention of cutting off their retreat. While one part of her admired the remarkable horsemanship she was observing, Abbie rode with her pistol raised and, drawing near to the two warriors, she chanced a snap shot, which sent one of the pair of braves reeling and ultimately falling under his horse's hoofs, while Dick Wootton dealt with the other in a similar fashion.

Jack had felt uneasy that morning and had kept the wagons closed up rather than letting them straggle along the trail each at his own speed. When he heard three shots way off in the distance, he acted swiftly, dividing the column into two and having the last four wagons brought up alongside the first four, with Jacob Levy's cart blocking the rear.

Due to the narrowness of the trail, it was impossible to actually circle the wagons. All he could do was create an elongated ellipse with the livestock in the middle. The two lead wagons were angled together, the next four slightly further apart, two on each side, and the final two four-wheeled vehicles again angled in with Jacob at the back.

This was not a spontaneous idea of Jack's. He, Abbie and Dick Wootton had planned this system from the time that the wagon train had left Fountain Creek, and all the people knew what to do. Thus, upon hearing the signal, the defence plan was immediately implemented and, by the time the two scouts hove in sight, together with their unwelcome followers, all was done to present a stern opposition to any would-be attackers.

Rapidly approaching the wagons, Abbie and Dick each steered their horses to the left and the right sides of the trail, leaving a clear field of fire for the wagon defenders to shoot at their pursuers. Jack had positioned himself and four of the best rifle shots at what he termed the spearhead of his ellipse, and directly their two fleeing companions got out of the way, he ordered independent fire at the approaching Indians. Four of the Comanche fell, as did three of their horses, which in turn caused a pile-up of the remainder on the narrow trail. This gave the resisters time to reload as Jack drew more defenders up to the spear-point so that continuous fire was brought to bear upon the screaming attackers.

Abbie rode parallel to the wagons and, spotting a gap, steered her bay who leapt over a tongue and stacked boxes into the enclosure, landing amid the milling and lowing livestock. Slipping from the saddle and grabbing her Springfield, she pushed her way forward to the spearhead to add to the deadly fire being delivered to the Comanche.

By now these had disentangled themselves and were again pressing home their attack upon the wagon train. There was once more a furious charge towards the wagons, which was repelled by the blistering fire coming from the defenders. There then followed a lull as the Comanche fell back out of rifle range and a figure mounted on a white horse appeared to be giving them a series of fresh orders.

'Let me see your telescope, Abbie! I'll see if I can recognize that varmint.'

Abbie retrieved her father's 'scope from the saddle of the bay and handed it to Dick Wootton, who levelled it at the distant hostiles.

'Why that's old Iron Shirt himself! I'd know that old devil anywhere! Here, take a look, Abbie!'

Abbie took the proffered telescope and peered through it at the mounted chief. She saw an imposing figure, gesticulating as if emphasizing the orders that he was giving to his warriors. He was clad in white buckskins, wearing a full war bonnet, and both his face and that of his horse were liberally daubed with painted symbols. The one aspect that was totally different from the garb of any Indians that she had seen to date was the polished iron breastplate that he wore and which was quite definitely not of native workmanship, but was probably very old and originally the property of some Spanish conquistador.

Abbie turned to Jack Harding, 'Jack! I understand you were the best shot in your regiment. How about demonstrating your skill with that Enfield of yours with a shot at old Iron Shirt?'

Jack smiled at her recognition of his marksmanship and nodded, 'Very well, Miss Abbie! I'll 'ave a go!'

He adjusted his sights to the full eight hundred-yard graduation and rested the fore end of his rifle on the side of a wagon. Pulling his hat down slightly to shade his eyes, he established a comfortable grip and, drawing the stock against his shoulder, he sighted and squeezed his trigger.

112

The Enfield barked but, at that very moment, Iron Shirt's horse moved slightly and the shot, which had been aimed at the centre of his breast plate, struck more of a glancing blow towards the left side, making a deep furrow but not quite penetrating. The blow, however, was sufficient to knock Iron Shirt from his horse and he lay on the ground with one arm feebly waving, proof that the shot had not proved fatal.

That one rifle shot had been enough for both the chief and his followers. They had already lost more than ten of their number, and Jack's shot convinced them that this wagon train was not worth the casualties they would incur to mount a successful attack. Therefore, they gathered up both their dead and wounded braves and, with two men supporting the injured chief, they departed from this place of Comanche defeat.

The small garrison waited cautiously, hardly daring to hope that they had beaten off an attack of the dreaded Comanche. Finally Dick Wootton set out to follow the trail of the defeated tribesmen and ensure that they were in truth leaving the area, and that their departure was not a wily trick. A couple of hours later he returned and reported that their enemy had indeed gone. Jack and Dick's two teamsters immediately took a team of oxen forward and dragged the dead horses some way off the trail so that the wagons could safely pass. All were hitched up and the caravan continued on its way north.

CHAPTER FOURTEEN

The rest of the journey to Colorado City was relatively uneventful, apart from a flash flood that threatened to sweep away three of the wagons, and an inquisitive bear that came snuffling around the camp seeking food but instead received a well-aimed shot to the head delivered by none other than Jacob Levy. Jacob was the hero of the hour and understandably basked in his brief blaze of glory. The bear meanwhile, skinned and dressed, was the central figure at a camp feast the next night.

The wagon train made camp on the outskirts of the community then describing itself as Colorado City, mainly because it was believed that the Colorado River begun in the vicinity. (At that time the area was still part of West Kansas and it wasn't until 1861 that Colorado Territory was actually formed.)

That night Abbie gathered all the people together.

'Friends, our journey together has ended. I said that I would be captain of this wagon train until our destination was reached, and this has been done. I suggest, however, that it might be a good idea for you to remain as a body while you explore the prospects in this area. I know of course that some of you have already got your plans laid, and I wish you well. For the others, well, if I can be of assistance in any way do not hesitate to approach me.'

Dick Wootton spoke up and proposed a vote of thanks to Miss Abbie for the way she had shouldered the burden of leadership as captain, and then went on, 'In one of my wagons I have two casks of Taos Lightning, which I will be taking with me up to Auraria. I also have a small keg of extra fine liquor which I think should be broached to celebrate this evening!'

A cheer went up as the keg was brought and people hurried to find mugs, tin cups and even pannikins with which to secure their share of the beverage. When all were drinking their fill, another person rose to address the assembly. Jacob Levy spoke of his despair when he had been thrown off his previous wagon train and the way that Abbie and everyone else had accepted him as one of the group. He stated that, although he would be leaving in the morning, they would always have a place in his heart.

He sat down and others expressed similar sentiments as the evening wore on. Finally the campfire died down and folks started wandering off to their wagons. Abbie stood for a few minutes, staring down at the red dying embers and thinking of all the strange twists and turns her life had taken since she had left India, when she was brought back to the present by a polite cough. 'S'cuse us, Miss Abbie! Could we 'ave a word or two with you?'

Abbie turned and saw in the moonlight Jack Harding and Dora McAdam standing there shyly holding hands and waiting for permission to speak. 'Jack and Dora! Not away to your beds yet? What did you wish to say to me?'

Jack shuffled his feet, looked at Dora for support, but she remained mute, and so finally he said, 'Well, Abbie, it's like this. Several times at night we've seen yer sitting by yerself looking over some papers an' stuff, as though you've got a problem. Now, me and Dora ain't made any firm plans yet, 'part from wanting to get 'itched, but we thought maybe we should stand by 'case you needed some 'elp. We've got a few dollars put by so we don't need to get jobs immediately. Watcha say? We don't mean to interfere with yer personal business!' Jack added hastily, concerned that he may have given offence.

Abbie smiled, shook her head and, reaching forward, she grasped both of them by the hand, 'No offence taken, dear friends! It is getting late now. Let me think over your very kind offer and it may be that tomorrow I can enlighten you regarding my little problem. Now is the time for beds. Or is it bed?' she added laughing, as she turned away to where her blanket roll awaited her.

Abbie lay awake thinking over Jack's offer. She did not know if the investigation regarding her father's investments constituted any danger and she certainly did not want to put her friends into any perilous situations. On the other hand, it would be good if there were others with whom she could share her knowledge and, if one of the supposed investments proved profitable, why she would be more than willing to share the wealth with such loyal friends. And with this last thought in her mind Abbie rolled over and went to sleep.

*

116

The next morning there were farewells as Dick Wootton, Jacob Levy and another wagon belonging to Naomi Johnson and Eve Schultz pulled out, and the remaining ones were deserted as their owners went into Colorado City seeking employment or information. Seeing that they had the campsite to themselves, Abbie got together with Jack and Dora and gave them a thorough account of her background and showed them the papers of her father's investments.

Initially, Jack was overcome by the thought that for weeks they had travelled, and been on the friendliest terms, with a real titled lady, and his early upbringing in England prompted him to start acting in an overly deferential manner.

Abbie pulled him up short, 'Look here, Jack Harding! Don't you go all silly on me! Next thing, you'll be tugging your forelock every time you open your mouth. This is the United States of America. We're all equal here, so I'm told! Dora, make that man of yours behave himself.

'Now down to business. I have three names here. The first is a young lawyer, Daniel Clifford. I'm going to see if I can locate him and gain an interview. Dora, would you make discreet enquiries about my father's agent, George Gillis, and his fatal accident. Be careful though! We don't know what happened to Mr Gillis. Jack, you're new in town. You're seeking employment. Find out what you can about this Roger Fenton. Is he operating a mine or a horse ranch in the area? If not, who is handling these concerns? That is, if they still exist. Just be very, very cautious, both of you. We'll compare notes over our evening meal.'

Abbie saddled her bay and rode into Colorado City.

Like so many small western towns of the period, the settlement presented an untidy appearance of unpainted clapboard shacks, log cabins with sod roofs and one rut-filled main street, with a number of false-fronted buildings, along the breadth of which was an uneven boardwalk.

The young girl seated astride a high-spirited gelding didn't attract too much attention until she halted by a general store, swung down and tied her horse to the hitching rail. Then the town loungers noticed the big pistol hanging butt forward on her left side, complemented by the large Bowie on her right hip, and an excited murmur ran through the crowd, 'Who is she? Looks like she's loaded for bear!'

Abbie entered the store and walked up to the counter to be greeted by an affable bald-headed man.

'Howdy, ma'am! What can I do for you?'

She didn't really need to buy anything, but did want to engage the storekeeper in a little light conversation hoping thereby to obtain information. So extracting a 12mm cartridge from the pouch at her belt, she held it out for inspection, 'Would you have any of these in stock?'

Benson, the storekeeper, took the proffered cartridge cautiously and held it up to the lamplight, 'No, I don't think so! What is it?'

Abbie patiently explained the type of pistol she was carrying and the function of the pinfire cartridge.

'Well, what do you know? The things they're bringing out these days!' He shook his head. 'Nope! I've never had call for that kind of load. Tell you what. There's a gentleman comes in here sometimes. He's a foreign guy who can

118

probably tell you all you need to know. Trouble is, you never know when he'll be in town, but I know he'll help you. Just ask for Mr Fenton.'

His listener suppressed a surge of excitement. 'Fenton, you say? Does he live around here?'

Mr Benson lost no time in expanding Abbie's knowledge of one who was a steady customer of his store.

'Why Mr Fenton is a big swell in these parts. He owns about half the town. Has a big horse ranch and also operates the Lucky Strike mine to the west of Pike's Peak. In fact,' he confided, 'Mr Fenton owns the land my store is sitting on.'

'Thank you, sir, for the information!' said Abbie. 'Just one thing more. Is there a lawyer by the name of Clifford, Daniel Clifford, in town here?'

The storekeeper's face lost its affable smile and he assumed a vague air, 'Clifford, eh? Clifford? Well, there was a young fella of that name here some time back. Before my time here,' he hastened to add. 'Understand he had a fatal accident. Horse fell on him. That's all I know. Sorry, can't help you any more.'

And he turned away and busied himself rearranging the rear shelves.

Abbie, realizing that her query about Clifford seemed to arouse suspicion, quickly said, 'Oh well, it's of no matter. There'll be lawyers in Auraria when I get there. My late grandfather always said, "Wherever you go, my girl, always have a lawyer handy. They're useful to know." And I've always tried to adhere to his advice. Goodbye, Mr Benson!'

So saying, Abbie left the store and stood on the sidewalk considering her next move while Benson continued to work on his shelves as he thought about his customer's last remark. 'Always have a lawyer handy. Silly woman!' and he dismissed her comment from his mind.

As Abbie stood undecided by the hitching rail, she felt a light tug on her left sleeve. She turned and found a scruffy, ragged little man standing there with a currying comb in his hand.

'Take yer hoss to the livery stable, miss! I'll curry him and give him a bait of oats. All for a quarter.'

As he made this offer, he pointed out the livery building further along on the same side where they were standing, and he gave a mysterious wink.

Abbie was very curious about the little man's optical gesture and so she permitted him to take the bay while she walked slowly along the boardwalk, ignoring the stares and whispered comments about the pistol-clad female. She walked past the livery and peeped in to where the little man was diligently currying the bay down. Seeing her, he beckoned urgently, 'I was in the store when you was talking to ol' Benson. That lawyer fella was always good to me. He died wi' a bullet in his back. They all said his hoss fell on him, but I know better, 'cos I heard 'em a-talking about it.'

Suddenly he continued in a loud voice, 'There y'are, miss. All nicely brushed and curried! Afternoon Mr Bradshaw, sir. Curry yer hoss? Old Joey always does a good job.'

The tall burly stranger who had approached so silently that Abbie had hardly heard his footsteps dismissed Joey's offer with a wave of his hand.

'Don't be givin' money to this barfly, lady! It'll just go

down his throat in liquid form. You're new in town, I believe?'

While saying this, Bradshaw was looking Abbie up and down with bold hot looks that made her feel unclean, as though his hairy hands were undressing her. She turned away without replying and walked quickly out into the street.

Behind her the coarse rough voice cried out, 'Hold on, you! I ain't finished talkin' to you yet! Wait up I say!' And, with an audible curse, Bart Bradshaw thrust Joey to one side, so violently that the little man fell into a stall, and strode out after Abbie.

She was crossing the street when he again ordered her to stop and, pulling his pistol, he put a shot into the ground close to her feet. Abbie stopped, and turned to face him.

'That's better! When I say stop, I damn' well mean it!' As Bradshaw said this, he was walking towards her, still with his right hand gripping the butt of his now sheathed revolver.

Abbie raised her left hand and cried out, 'Stop! You are obviously looking for trouble. Well, now you've found it. Draw!'

As she said these last words, Abbie dropped into a crouch, with her right hand hovering above her cross-draw pistol. Bart Bradshaw seemed to finally realize that the unknown woman was not playing a flirtatious game with him, and frantically started to clear his gun from its holster.

As he did so, Abbie drew in one fluid motion. The left hand grasped her gun ahead of the trigger-guard, as she

121

thumbed back the hammer and fired at her opponent. Her first bullet hammered into his right shoulder, above the armpit, tearing apart flesh and muscle, before exiting through Bart's shoulder blade. Her second deliberately-aimed shot smashed into his kneecap, dropping him to the ground. As he scrabbled frantically in the dust for his fallen Colt, Abbie walked swiftly forward, kicked his gun to one side, and stuck her pinfire revolver right between his eyes with the hot muzzle touching his flesh.

Terrified, he stared up at her in agony because of his wounds, but petrified, not daring to move, in case that cocked hammer six inches from his skull should fall and thereby end his earthly existence.

'Now, you miserable creature! You thought that you could run roughshod over all that you meet, and especially treat any woman as a mere chattel. Now you've had a lesson to remember all of your life. And if you want to know who your teacher was, I'm known as "The Pinfire Lady"!'

She holstered her pistol and turned away.

Approaching her from the main saloon waddled a corpulent figure sporting a five-pointed star on his dirty vest. 'I'll take that pistol, young woman! We don't allow wanton shooting of innocent citizens in my town!' And he held out his hand expectantly for Abbie's revolver.

She carefully drew the pinfire, holding it with one finger and thumb, and reached forward with it, then, just as Billy Curtis had taught her, operated the Border Roll, so that the Town Marshal suddenly found the unwelcome sensation of a 12mm barrel pressing more than gently against his navel. 'Not this time, Marshal! What kind of a city do you run here where decent women cannot walk the streets without being accosted? The man I shot drew his pistol first on me. I merely reacted to a situation not of my choosing.'

Marshal Henry Firman was not a brave man and had no intention of being a hero. He blustered. He made references to city ordinances, but all the while he was searching for a way to back down without losing too much face. He was saved by the fact that a large number of citizens came up and corroborated Abbie's story, allowing him to mutter something about being perhaps mistaken, hoping all would help him keep the peace.

As he turned away, one of the gathered crowd said mockingly, 'Off you go, Henry, like a good boy. Make your report to Roger Fenton when he comes to town. Maybe he'll buy you a lollipop!' at which remark a number of those present broke into jeering laughter. A couple of the more compassionate men assisted the groaning Bradshaw to a shack, which constituted the surgery and living quarters of Dr Stevens, the only medical man within thirty miles.

As Marshal Firman slunk off, the folks left gathered around Abbie, curious about her gunplay skills. Yet being westerners, they hesitated to speak up and intrude on her privacy.

'Well, good people, I'm really sorry to introduce myself in such a violent manner, but I felt that I had very little choice.'

A voice in the crowd spoke up with, 'Don't you worry about Bart Bradshaw, ma'am. Ol' Bart's been pushing his weight around here too long and he was due for a fall.'

There were murmurs of agreement at this remark, followed by someone else noting that Roger Fenton was the only man likely to miss Bradshaw. Others asked Abbie what type of gun she carried and where she had learned to shoot, but to all queries she just gave vague replies. Finally she held up a hand for silence.

'Now I have a question of you gentlemen! Where can a lady get a decent meal and a cup of coffee in Colorado City?'

There was movement in the crowd as a tall, well-built and elegantly-dressed man pushed his way forward. Sweeping off his wide brimmed hat and bowing low, he declaimed, 'Arnold Le Clair at your service, ma'am. Allow me the honour of escorting you to our finest eating establishment, namely the Café Royale, although I am assured that its owner is in fact a staunch Republican.'

Abbie looked at him with that frank gaze that so many men found to be so disconcerting. She saw a dark-complexioned man with a thin moustache and even features that would have made him positively handsome were it not for the livid scar on one cheek. He looked at her with a disarming smile and remarked, 'Well! Are you satisfied with the inspection?'

Abbie thanked him prettily for his invitation and, taking his offered arm, they walked along the boardwalk, trailed by a goodly number of the admiring crowd, to the Café Royale where the two customers were presented with, and consumed, a meal worthy of a Parisian Café.

CHAPTER FIFTEEN

Arnold was a delightful table companion. He had travelled considerably both in North America and in Europe and had an extensive repertoire of amusing tales with which to regale his fellow diner. Abbie noticed with a certain amusement that most of his selected stories seemed to be presented with a view to drawing out responses from her that would furnish him with more information about herself.

Abbie decided that it would do no harm to prick Arnold's self-confidence a little as he seemed set on impressing her with his worldly air. Early on in their conversation, he had admitted quite frankly that he was a professional gambler, and so now during a break in Arnold's discourse she put down her silverware, looked at him intently and said, 'Arnold, do you know it really seems very strange sitting here with you, a professional gambler. Did you ever meet a certain Paul LaRue?'

He frowned a little at her question and responded, 'Paul LaRue? Why yes, we've played cards together. Why do you ask?'

'Well,' replied Abbie slowly, 'I didn't really get to know the man myself. We only met once and I shot him – in a duel!'

Arnold's jaw dropped and he looked at her in disbelief. Despite the fact that scarcely an hour ago she had shot the town bully, Bart Bradshaw, he hadn't been able to rid himself of the notion that her victory was somehow a fluke. And here she was calmly telling him that she had had a formal duel with a noted gunman and had won.

In the silence that followed, Abbie thought that it would do no harm to give Arnold a very brief outline of some of her experiences, including her role as wagon captain, the fight with Scar and his gang and a couple of her other gunfights, with the result that Arnold Le Clair was bewildered by this seemingly accomplished Victorian lady who was also a deadly gunfighter.

The meal was finished and they spontaneously rose from the table. Abbie insisted on paying her share of the bill; she didn't want to be beholden to anyone. 'That was an excellent meal, Mr Le Clair, and delightful conversation. Now I must be collecting my horse from the livery stable and heading back to our wagon site.'

She felt there was no need to inform Le Clair that her wagon train had broken up. He might well be friendly, but she had learned to be cautious.

They parted at the door to the café and Abbie walked down to the livery stable, receiving respectful acknowledgments from the people on the boardwalk. Her bay was inside, all groomed, fed and ready to go. Joey waited expectantly for his fee and Abbie produced a dollar, which she held out in one hand. 'Joey! Before I give you this dollar, I want you to repeat what you were saying to me when we were so rudely interrupted by Bart Bradshaw.'

Joey eyed the dollar and licked his lips nervously, 'Well, ma'am, I usually sleep in a stall or up in the loft if old Wilson, that's the owner, ain't mad at me. This particular night I was up in the loft when Mr Bradshaw brought a horse back in. It had been rented earlier in the day by Mr Clifford. Bradshaw said to two men waiting for him, "Well, it's done! He wasn't expecting anything. The bullet hit him in the back, right between the shoulder blades. Give me a hand, fellas! There's blood all over this saddle." The three of them cleaned up the saddle and brushed old Bob down. Then they left, taking Bob with them. The next morning he was found wandering outside the town and a search party found Mr Clifford's body lying on the edge of an arroyo. To make it seem like a robbery, his pockets were turned inside out. That's all I know, ma'am.'

'Thank you Joey, here's the dollar. By the way! Did you recognize the two men?'

'One was that Roger Fenton. I dunno who the other was. Take care, ma'am.' And Joey scuttled off, the dollar clutched in his hand.

Abbie climbed into the saddle and rode slowly out of Colorado City. Reaching the wagon site, she found several others of her party had returned with mixed impressions about their job-seeking experiences. Bobby Smith had been told that Fenton who owned the Lucky Strike mine wasn't taking on any new hands. He was advised to try other mining ventures in the area.

Ann Marlowe and Beth Isaacson had found an empty

127

store, which they thought would be ideal for the kind of snack bar they had been considering. Now they had to work out a deal with the present owner. Meanwhile they intended to remain at the present campsite where there were folks that they knew.

As Abbie stood chatting with her wagon train friends, Jack Harding rode in pulling a long face and shrugging his shoulders in response to her silent query. The group split up and both Abbie and Jack started preparing the evening meal for the three of them. The food was cooked and the coffee boiling away before Dora stumbled into camp. Her shirtwaist was torn at the shoulder, her bonnet was all awry, and she presented a dishevelled appearance. She sank down on a box and gratefully sipped at a mug of coffee offered by Abbie while Jack hovered around anxiously awaiting Dora's story of how she got in such a condition.

At length Dora had recovered her composure and narrated how she had walked into town and had decided to start her enquiries at the bank. There was only a young teller in evidence and when she enquired about George Gillis, he gave conflicting answers. Initially he stated that the bank could not reveal any information regarding customers. This statement was then modified when he admitted to Dora that Mr Gillis was dead, but no, he did not know how it happened. It was before his time at the bank. He suggested Dora try the main General Store.

She had gone as directed and met the affable Mr Benson; affable, that is, until she explained that a friend back east had asked her to find out about the fatal accident experienced by a certain Mr Gillis. Directly she had mentioned the name, Benson's manner changed. He became flustered. He blustered and finally asked to be excused for a few minutes as he had to deliver an outstanding order. He left by a back door and fifteen minutes later had not returned.

Dora had waited patiently, but was about to leave when a man entered the store. He was of medium height, had a well-trimmed Louis Napoleon beard, was well dressed and, like most men, was wearing a gun belt. He had smiled disarmingly at Dora and said that he understood that she was making enquiries about poor Mr Gillis. He had then suggested that it was not a subject to discuss standing at a store counter, and invited her to accompany him to his office behind the Bonanza Saloon of which he was the owner.

Dora had gone with him, her companion chatting in the most friendly fashion, as they walked the short distance to the saloon. He kept apologizing, because they had to walk through the empty barroom to get to his office. He had opened the door and ushered her in. Directly she was in his office cum living quarters, his manner changed and he had thrown her down upon a couch, demanding to know what her interest was in the late George Gillis. She had jumped up and demanded to leave. Her captor had grabbed and in the ensuing struggle her clothing was torn. Just as she was down on the couch once more, there came a hammering at the door and a voice calling out for Marty. His response for the caller to go away just invited more hammering and the remark that Bart was having a problem.

Marty, the bearded one, got up and, threatening Dora

with a dog whip hanging on the wall, he went out locking the door behind him. She tried the door. It was solid. There was no chance of shaking the lock loose. The one grimy window in the room was in the wall facing an alley. It was of the sash type where the lower half slid up to double the top portion. The window was locked with a swivel catch and Dora thought that, given time, she could maybe loosen the rusted parts.

Taking a nail file from her reticule, with heart hammering, she set to work scraping away at the rusty paint-encrusted catch. Time passed, there seemed little noise coming from the barroom and fortunately Marty did not put in an appearance. Finally, the catch was clear of rust and paint, but still would not turn. Dora saw she needed some kind of leverage and looked around. The dog whip might serve the purpose and, seizing it, she used the handle to force the catch to turn. Slowly it began to move until the lower portion of the sash widow was free to ride up when pushed from below. The window rose about two inches and stuck; and that was the situation when a funny little man appeared, looking in at her. He saw Dora's predicament and, putting a finger to his lips, he vanished, reappearing with a piece of board which he employed to pry the stuck window up and then helped Dora climb through into the alley. Thanking her rescuer, and eliciting the fact that his name was Joey, Dora had hurried to get safely back to the wagons.

Abbie and Jack looked at each other and at the still shaken Dora. There was a long silence, broken by Jack who declared; 'I think I'd better pay Mr Marty whatever his name is a little visit and teach 'im some manners! 'E doesn't go around treating any lady like that, let alone my girl!'

'Hold on, Jack! I'm just as indignant as you over the treatment Dora experienced, but we don't want to go off at half cock. I think that we have to consider where we stand before we make the next move. Don't worry though. In time Marty will receive his just desserts.'

Abbie's remarks were echoed by Dora who suggested that next time she would be more careful and less trusting before allowing herself to be in effect sweet-talked into a dangerous situation.

The trio decided to see what they had accomplished by their foray into Colorado City.

'Well!' listed Abbie, 'We know that the storekeeper Benson appears to take his orders from somebody else and that he doesn't own his establishment. We also have experienced that the names of both Gillis and Clifford get a negative reaction. The man Marty would definitely appear to be one of the enemy as would the town marshal, Henry Firman. From remarks made by bystanders, both apparently take orders from the mysterious Roger Fenton who, so far, has not appeared on the scene.

'I'm not sure about the gambler, Le Clair. He was certainly probing during the meal that I had with him but, then again, it may well have been mere professional curiosity.'

Dora interjected, 'The little man Joey would seem to be on our side. At least, that was my feeling when he helped me escape.'

Abbie endorsed Dora's opinion, suggesting that another chat with Joey would be a good idea. And on that note they prepared to bed down for the night with the understanding that they would pursue the mystery further in the morning.

CHAPTER SIXTEEN

The next day, leaving Jack and Dora with the wagons, Abbie rode into town. She visited other establishments, such as the other general store, more struggling but seemingly more patronized than that of Mr Benson. There was a ladies' haberdashery that warranted a visit, not with the notion that she might gain information, but rather because that was what she was expected to do. Actually, it was a worthwhile visit. The Misses Partridge who ran the haberdashery were two middle-aged ladies who had originally hailed from Dover in Kent, England, and were absolutely enthralled to have somebody to chat to from the country that they had left so long ago. She was invited back for a longer visit, at which time they intended to tell her the adventures that had led them to Colorado City. At least, that was their intent if they were still there. That man Fenton, their landlord, was unlike dear Mr Gillis, their first landlord, who had been so understanding. Fenton demanded his rent on the first Monday of the month and was always threatening to close them down. At length

Abbie posed a question regarding the fate of poor Mr Gillis.

Both sisters replied describing how the Gillis riderless horse had come into town and how his body was found several days later in an arroyo where he had been evidently thrown from his steed. That is what the marshal said in his report to the City Council. The body had been buried in the little cemetery outside the city limits. Most people attended and the grave was still looked after by Joey the ostler.

'Hmm,' thought Abbie. 'That's interesting that Joey's name should come up in conversation. I think that I'll have to try and have a conversation with that gentleman.'

She purchased a few small items from the two sisters who seemed grateful for the sale and took her leave.

Acting on the directions she had just received, Abbie rode out to the sadly neglected Boot Hill. Neglected that is except for one grave. She dismounted and, loosely tethering her bay, she strolled around the little graveyard, stopping at various mounds to read the fading inscriptions on sagging wooden crosses and the odd weathered monument. Deliberately Abbie kept her movements casual so that if anyone was spying on her he would be unable to see if she paid more attention to any one inscription. She walked by the grave of Daniel Clifford, already overgrown, and just as quickly passed that of George Gillis, noticing out of the corner of her eye how neat it was with a jar of wilting flowers close to the simple wooden cross.

Back in the saddle Abbie rode back through town watching to see if Joey was around. As she was passing Marty's Bonanza saloon, a man stepped off the boardwalk and accosted her, 'Heh, you! I want to talk to you!'

Abbie reined in the bay and looked down at the fellow who addressed her in such a rough coarse manner.

'Are you speaking to me?' she responded in a cold imperious tone, deliberately remaining aloof.

'Yeah! I'm talking to you! Who d'ya think you are shooting one of my men down in the street without any reason or provocation?'

'Well, I most certainly know who I am, but who do you think you are, addressing me in this uncouth manner? What's your name?'

'My name's Roger Fenton! Bart Bradshaw was one of my top hands and it happens that I own most of Colorado City! I demand to know what gives you the right to come here and go around deliberately stirring up trouble.'

'Oh!' replied Abbie. 'So you are *that* Roger Fenton! The one who seems to have obtained all of these properties in some suspicious manner. So folks are saying up and down the Mountain Branch trail.'

As she spoke the last remark, Abbie deliberately raised her voice for the benefit of the people gathered on the boardwalk listening with a certain amount of pleasure to the altercation between the Pinfire Lady and the boss of Colorado City who had frequently made life uncomfortable and uncertain for many of them.

Completing her statement, Abbie spurred the bay forward, almost trampling Fenton underfoot and rode back to the wagons. As she neared the encampment, she saw a knot of people amongst whom were Jack Harding and three men wearing large Mexican sombreros. She reined in the bay and dismounted. One of the Mexicans

135

came forward, taking off his hat.

'*Buenas noches, señorita*! Do you remember me? It is Miguel. Miguel Garcia, Mr Bent's *hombre*. Mr Bent, he has a big package for the *señorita*, and he say for Miguel to bring it, but to have two guards cos they are ver' bad *hombres* on the trail. So,' introducing his companions, 'I bring Pedro and José with me!'

Both of the other two Mexicans removed their sombreros and bowed low to Abbie, who acknowledged them with a large smile. 'And what have you got for me, Miguel, that prompted such a long perilous journey?'

Miguel indicated the two large packages still lashed either side of a patient pack mule. 'Here are the bullets for *La Señorita*'s Pinfire gun that Mr Bent he order fro New York! Mr Bent, he also say we three to stay with the *señorita* as long as she need us! Is that OK?'

Abbie indicated her pleasure at their arrival and said they were most welcome to stay, although it was possible that there could be trouble in the near future. The mule was unpacked and Abbie, with Jack's assistance, carefully opened up one of the wooden packing cases. Inside the case were ten cardboard boxes, each containing twenty-five 12mm pinfire cartridges.

She unloaded her pistol and reloaded with five of the new cartridges. They fitted perfectly and, walking a short way from the wagons, she discharged her pinfire against a convenient tree. The five shots rang out and Abbie nodded in satisfaction. The powder load seemed the same as the ones she had been using, but which, of late, she had to use sparingly, as she had fewer than forty left.

Over their evening meal Abbie related what she had

136

learned and experienced that day and remarked that Roger Fenton must be getting agitated about the recent enquiries as he seemed to be showing his less than pleasant self in his dealings with the newcomers.

As the group sat chatting around the campfire in the soft evening air, another figure loomed up out of the darkness. It was little Joey, out of breath, indicating that he had been running fast and that his visit was urgent. He sought out Abbie in the firelight and, apologizing for breaking in on their evening's rest, he burst out with, ''Scuse me, ma'am, but this is terribly important. Old Fenton has got some of his men together in town an' they're agonna pretend they're Injuns an' attack your camp later tonight! I thought I'd better warn you! They mean business!'

Abbie immediately took command of the situation. 'Thank you, Joey, it might be better if you stay here. Jack, get everyone together so we can inform them of the problem. Then get the men to start rolling these wagons together to provide a better defence. Miguel, this is not your fight. If you wish to leave, we won't hold it against you. On the other hand, if you wish to stay and help us defend the wagon camp, you and your *compadres* will be more than welcome.'

Miguel, Pedro and José all expressed a desire to join in the defence. The people were gathered round and the situation was explained to them. In addition to Jack and Dora, the three Mexicans and herself, there was Bobby Smith and his mother, Beth Isaacson and Ann Marlowe and two men who had joined the wagon train at Fountain Creek. That gave them a total of twelve defenders, all of whom were reasonably good shots, and a quick survey indicated that there was an ample supply of both powder and shot.

Abbie left it up to Jack to spread the people around the defence perimeter and to ensure that buckets of water were standing ready in case the counterfeit Indians attempted to set the wagons on fire.

While all these arrangements were being made, Abbie had a long talk with the man who had just warned them of the forthcoming attack, 'Joey, I want you to tell me all you can about Mr Gillis and also Mr Clifford.'

'Well, ma'am, Mr Gillis came to Colorado City about the same time as I did. He was a real swell, being an agent for some Englishman who had invested a lot of money in the area. Me? I was just a nobody, bin kicked off a wagon train 'cos I had no money. That didn't matter to Mr Gillis. He always treated me just like you would regular folks. Gave me little jobs to do, and little errands to run. He always said I was his general ... general ... what's the word? I know. His general factotum. He promised that later, when he was fully settled, he'd have a regular job for me.

'Then he went missing. His horse came back without him, and a few days later his body was found in an arroyo. That there marshal, Henry Firman, said his horse had rolled on him or had thrown him. The story seemed to change, an' no wonder. The chestnut that came back with an empty saddle was not the one that he'd ridden off on. Close, mind you. Very close. But I'd know old Brownie anywhere. I'd groomed her enough times!

'Well, anyway, that Roger Fenton turned up and said he

was authorized to handle all the investment holdings that Mr Gillis had looked after. Then Daniel Clifford came to the city. He questioned the legal rights of Fenton and actually challenged him to prove his case. They were in that office where Miss Dora was held. I was underneath. (I sometimes check the crawlspace under the saloon looking for coins that customers drop accidentally through the cracks in the floorboards.) Well, anyway, I heard them talking, and Mr Clifford said that he had definite proof about all the property rights. Fenton indicated that he had to go out to his ranch but, being a reasonable man, he would be delighted if Mr Clifford could come out that evening and show him the papers.

'Well, I quietly left from the rear of the saloon and went back to the livery stable. Early that evening, Mr Clifford came for a horse. He had a small leather satchel with him and was wearing a gun belt. Now that was mighty strange, as he'd never worn one before. Before he left he said to me, "Joey you've always done a good job for me! I like the way you still look after Mr Gillis' grave; continue to care for it. Promise?" I promised and he left. The rest I already told you.'

As Joey completed his narration, there was a low call from Jack Harding. 'Stand to, everyone! We have unwelcome visitors.'

Telling Joey to stay under cover, Abbie seized her Springfield rifle and ran to her allotted defence position, already occupied by Ann Marlow and Beth Isaacson. In the bright light of a nearly full moon, she saw a number of riders, possibly more than a dozen bunched together as they received their final instructions. The bunch broke apart and spread out into a line with some of the riders carrying lighted torches.

At a given signal they began to move forward, their pace quickly changing to a gallop as they swept down upon the supposedly sleeping camp. At the same time the night air was filled with hideous yells and screams as the raiders attempted to emulate a true war party. Jack Harding called out, 'Hold your fire! Let them get closer!'

Then as the horsemen got well within one hundred yards, the order rang out, 'Fire at will!'

Jack had positioned most of the rifles on the city side of the wagon train, making the logical assumption that this was the direction from which the attack would come and, at his order, a ripple of rifle shots rent the night air. The initial volley was followed by a flurry of pistol shots as those with side-arms aimed and fired them at the advancing enemy.

The result of the wagon defenders' fire was devastating. Fully half of the bare-chested white men, daubed with paint to suggest they were Indians, were either down and dismounted or lying motionless on the ground. The attack faltered and faded away as most of the survivors suddenly realized that this simple hoorah against unsuspecting settlers had turned into a disastrous defeat and they obviously believed that they had urgent business elsewhere.

Those dismounted, and still able to walk, turned and ran. Only two or possibly three attempted to press home the forlorn attack. One was opposite Abbie's position. Drawing her pinfire, she levelled it and, aiming with care, brought the rider down when he was but ten feet from the

140

wagon. With a 12mm ball in the centre of his chest, he fell, and his horse, relieved of the weight, trotted to a standstill and stood there motionless, as Jack called out, 'Cease fire!' followed by 'Reload!'

Silence fell upon the little battlefield. Silence, that is, apart from the groaning of wounded men and the shrill whinnying of crippled horses. After a short wait the defenders realized that there would not be a resumption of the pseudo-Indian attack and they walked out to aid the wounded and put the injured animals out of their misery.

Abbie walked forward and stared down at the man she had just shot with her pinfire. It was quite evident that his wound was fatal and she knelt down and stared into his pain-wracked features. He looked up at her and grimaced, 'Sorry, Abbie. I didn't think life would end like this. There was nothing personal. I just had a job to do, that's all.'

His head fell sideways and his eyes glazed over.

Abbie bit her lip as she looked down at the dead Arnold Le Clair, remembering the pleasant meal they had enjoyed together, and then she rose to her feet. Arnold had made his choice and, if the attack had been success-ful, it would have been her and possibly most of her friends who would have been lying dead in the warm summer's night. As it was the defenders had no casualties; they had been lucky.

Le Clair and the other three dead 'Indians' were loaded belly down on horses and Abbie, Jack and Miguel saddled their own animals and prepared to deliver the corpses to Colorado City. Abbie told Joey before they departed to slip unnoticed back to the livery stable. She would undoubtedly have need of him again. The wounded attackers were made as comfortable as possible until they could get Dr Stevens to come out to the wagon camp and Abbie and her companion left to deliver their gruesome cargo.

The solemn procession wended its way down the main street and halted in front of Marty's Bonanza saloon. The lights were on and there was activity inside, but nobody emerged to see what was going on in the street. Quietly the four corpses were unloaded from the horses and laid out in a line on the boardwalk. When the three were back in the saddle, Abbie pulled her pistol and fired three shots in the air. Inside the Bonanza, the piano stopped and the normal loud chatter fell silent. Then the batwing doors swung open and men headed by Marty spilled out, only to stop short at the bodies lying in front of them.

Abbie raised her voice. 'I understand that Mr Le Clair and his other associates lived here or close by. Perhaps you'll be good enough to give them burials. Unfortunately, they made very poor Indians. You might tell Mr Fenton that. We are sure that he will be interested.'

And with a mocking salute Abbie and her two companions swung round and galloped out of town.

CHAPTER SEVENTEEN

In the morning Bobby Smith was delegated to bring Dr Stevens out, and meanwhile Abbie, Jack and Dora held a council of war. Jack opened the debate with an observation that Roger Fenton was certainly going to react to the failure of his 'Indian' attack.

'Abbie, I'm sure there'll be another attack, if not against the wagons, but more likely against individuals in town.'

'That is what will most likely happen, Jack. I'm sure there are plenty of decent people in Colorado City. Somehow we've got to get more of them involved on our side.'

Dora spoke up, 'Look! Would the locals swing behind us if we could prove that Roger Fenton is an outright crook and has no legitimate claim to the properties in the city and beyond?'

Jack Harding nodded in agreement, 'That's right! Abbie, you were having a long chat with Joey just before the attack. Did you learn anything more?'

Abbie related the content of the conversation she had with the livery ostler, and the three of them sat silent in thought. Finally Jack looked up and said, ''Ere! What 'appened to the satchel that Daniel Clifford was carrying when 'e left to go to Fenton's ranch?'

'Well. . . .' Abbie paused. 'I suppose Fenton must have it hidden it away somewhere, or probably he destroyed it.'

Dora interjected excitedly, 'If he had it, he would have been waving those documents around just to prove he was the legitimate owner, but I'm certain that he wouldn't destroy land claims. I don't think that he ever got them.'

'Well where are they?' rejoined Jack. 'Abbie, tell us that last bit again!'

Abbie did so, and as she finished the three looked at each other and simultaneously cried out, 'The grave of George Gillis!'

Abbie continued, 'Clifford knew that he was making a dangerous visit to Fenton, that's why he was wearing a gun belt. He obviously didn't think that he'd be ambushed on the way there, but as a precaution, he may have buried the satchel in the grave and, to make sure nobody would suspect the hiding place, encouraged Joey to tend it and replace the flowers frequently. Since it is highly probable that Le Clair and company will be buried in the same graveyard, it might be a good idea to get over there now and see if our theory is correct. Come on, Jack!'

Leaving Miguel and Dora in charge of things at the wagon camp, Abbie and Jack rode to the little lonely over-grown Boot Hill. The place was deserted and Jack, taking the shovel they had brought with them, followed Abbie over to the grave of George Gillis. 'Jack, I suggest that we dig the area close to the headboard. Not too deep! Clifford quite probably did not have any tools with him. He probably used a stick or something to scrape away the dirt.'

Jack did as Abbie advised and, as he carefully turned over the topsoil, his efforts were almost immediately rewarded, as the edge of a leather object came into view. The earth was carefully cleared away and there lay Clifford's satchel, its leather damp and grimy, the steel protective corners red with rust and the brass hasp green with verdigris.

Abbie picked up the satchel and wiped it off with a riding glove. Having no key, she slipped her Bowie under the lock and twisted, prying the satchel open. Inside were packets of papers, carefully wrapped in oilskin which had preserved them from the elements. She opened one packet and the name Frederick Martin, her own father, stared up at her. They had found what they were looking for. Jack tidied the grave and they rode back to the wagons, jubilant that they had been successful in their quest.

Back at their camp, Abbie slipped from the saddle and walked over to where Dr Stevens was standing, sipping a welcome mug of coffee after patching up the wounded 'Indians'. He lowered his mug and looked at her quizzically. 'Ah! So here's the young lady who has been creating all the mayhem around here. The Pinfire Lady, I presume. Or would it be more correct to address you as . . .' he paused and looked at Abbie hard, 'Miss Martin? The daughter of the late Major Frederick Martin?'

Abbie took the hand the doctor offered and remarked, 'And you must be Dr Stevens, who apparently knows more about me than I do about him. Perhaps we may exchange information?'

Abbie too took a mug of coffee offered to her by Ann Marlowe and she and the doctor walked some little way and sat down on a fallen log. Dr Stevens explained how he had been a friend of both George Gillis and Daniel Clifford and in fact had actually met Major Martin, then a young lieutenant on an extended furlough and touring the West. From Gillis he had learned that Martin had a young daughter and had become a widower. He also had a rough notion of how Gillis had become Major Martin's agent in Colorado City and how Roger Fenton had ingratiated himself with the agent shortly after coming to work with him.

The death of George Gillis had appeared to be an accident and Fenton had indicated that he had written to England and was attending to affairs awaiting further instructions. Then gradually he had let it be known that he was assuming full ownership of the ranch and other properties.

Somehow Daniel Clifford got hold of all the deeds to the Martin holdings. 'I suspect that he may have raided Fenton's office in town since the latter suddenly moved everything out to the ranch. Daniel told me he had the papers and was going to challenge Fenton's legal position. That's really all I know.'

Abbie gave the doctor a brief outline of her autobiography from the time of her father's death to the present day, omitting only her marriage to Bertram Penraven, and produced adequate proof of her legitimate claims upon the Martin American estate. 'I think that it's time that a party of us paid a visit to Mr Fenton at my ranch. Care to accompany us, Doctor?'

'No, Abbie! I think that I've got a better idea. I believe that you, with enough documentation to prove your case and two or three of your people, should accompany me into Colorado City and I'll call an emergency meeting of the City Council. Get them on our side and the word will quickly spread among the folks that you're the legitimate owner of several of their respective establishments.'

Abbie saw the sense of Stevens's proposal and they rode into town together with Jack and Miguel to meet with the Council. Dr Stevens used his influence as the only medically qualified man in town to get the other members of the Council to attend a meeting at the community hall.

Within the hour the members were assembled, although more than one looked askance at the presence of Abbie and her two companions. Briefly Dr Stevens outlined the history of events up to and including the attack on the wagons and then invited Abbie to speak. She rose from her seat and in a clear voice described in detail her background and her relationship to the man who had owned most of the locations during the founding of Colorado City. She ended her explanation with the story of how Roger Fenton had in effect stolen all that he now possessed and had no right to be dominating the community and living off their profits.

There were nods of agreement at this last remark for all had felt economic pressure from Fenton and his cronies.

The only noises of dissent came from Marty Rudd, owner of the Bonanza saloon, and Howard Benson of the main general store. The third person who no doubt would have protested but didn't have a voice at the meeting was Marshal Henry Firman. He slipped out of the meeting when he saw the way things were moving and was reported to have left town in a hurry, no doubt to report to his master, Fenton.

Howard, in an unsteady voice, demanded proof that all was as Abbie had described. Jack handed Clifford's satchel to her and she produced documentary evidence that left the store-keeper silent and quaking in his seat as he came to the realization that the woman in front of him actually owned his business venture.

Rudd was far more hostile. 'Lady, you might have all these folks buffaloed but you don't have me worried none! Possession is nine tenths o' the law an' I've got a fair deal from Roger Fenton. He's gonna come into town and. . . .' he paused, 'when he's finished, things will be jus' as they were before 'cept you and your bunch won't be here!'

With that he kicked over his chair and stalked from the hall.

There was a long silence broken by Dr Stevens who rising remarked, 'And that's the way in which the bullies who have formerly run your lives have always behaved. Now their day is done, and by uniting behind Abbie Martin and the cause of justice we can rid this city of the blackguards who have hitherto made life miserable for so many people.'

A pair of female voices echoed the doctor's statement, 'Hear! Hear!' as the Partridge twins lent their shrill tones to the murmur of assent which had greeted the doctor's observation.

Abbie said that she would bring her wagons into town and pointed out that she could furnish at least a dozen riflemen and, if Colorado City could find an equal number, there should be no problem in repelling any attack by Fenton and his minions.

In an about-face, Howard Benson stood up and offered supplies of powder and shot, together with a small quantity of rifles from his stock. The wily Benson could see which way the wind was blowing.

Then it was proposed to form a town guard of all able-bodied men and Abbie suggested that it be put under the command of Jack Harding since he had military experience. This suggestion was heartily endorsed and by the time that the meeting was adjourned, measures were well underway to defend the city.

CHAPTER EIGHTEEN

Leaving Jack to start his recruiting drive, Abbie returned to the wagon camp and informed the folks of how the situation had evolved. She explained how in effect she had volunteered them to aid in the defence of Colorado City and suggested that they move all the wagons into town immediately.

Such was the trust that the individual people had in Abbie's leadership that not one questioned her, and all set to work hitching up their teams and preparing to move. For one last time Abbie looked back at a line of wagons, and mentally checking that all was ready called out, 'Wagons roll!' and the wagons moved the short distance along the trail to the main street where each was allocated space between the buildings on either side to act as an additional barrier to any would-be attackers.

Meanwhile Jack had been busy mustering his town guard and assigning them to defence positions along the street. While wanting to create a crossfire, Jack also wanted to ensure that the defenders positioned on both sides did not end up having a pitched battle between themselves.

Abbie signalled for Miguel to join her and walked over to Jack. 'Look! You have everything well in hand here. Miguel and I are going to ride out a couple of miles or so and scout around. I think that Fenton will try to strike quickly before he thinks we're ready for him. While we're gone, watch out for Marty Rudd. I don't trust him one little bit!'

Meanwhile, as all these defensive preparations were being made, Roger Fenton was gathering his forces together in an attempt to reassert his power and authority over Colorado City. When, as suspected by the observers, Marshal Henry Firman had fled the city, he had gone straight to inform Fenton of the change of power. Roger Fenton was furious. He went into a blind rage at the thought of his carefully constructed financial empire crashing down about him and was determined to win back all that he had unlawfully owned.

The ill-fated 'Indian' attack on the wagon camp had cost him quite a few of his best gun-hands and there was a need for more firepower. He therefore sent a message summoning the miners of the Lucky Strike mine to come armed immediately to the ranch for an emergency meeting. When they had assembled he addressed them, 'Men! You all know that I've always treated you square! Well, a sad situation has arisen. There's a woman in Colorado City who's goin' around telling the folks that she owns the mine an' that she's goin' ter close it down. That means you all will be out of work! Are we gonna let that happen?'

There was a resounding roar of 'No!' from the assembled workers, and forming into an armed column they, with the remaining gun-hands and Roger Fenton at their head, set out to march to Colorado City to seek vengeance upon any who were considering taking away their livelihood.

Abbie and Miguel spotted the column of men flowing over the brow of a hill about three miles from the city. 'Miguel! You continue to keep watch over them while I ride back and warn the folks that Fenton is coming on fast. So they had better be prepared. Be careful! Keep a good distance from them.'

'*Sí Señorita*! I will do this. An' I will ride quick when I think he is very close!'

Abbie turned the bay and rode swiftly back to Colorado City. Entering the main street and noting all the preparations for defence, she was surprised to see a stage coach drawn up outside Mrs O'Brien's Rooming House and a group of well-dressed people, presumably Easterners, standing on the boardwalk. She was even more surprised and excited to see a short, grey-bearded figure in buckskins, standing in the midst of the group, yet looking sadly out of place amid all the eastern finery.

With a loud cry of 'Billy!' Abbie threw herself from the saddle, and rushing over she grabbed her old mentor and seized him in a tight bear hug.

'Where on earth did you come from? What are you doing here? I must say you have chosen a great time to visit!' The words just spilled out of her, so pleased was she to see the old trapper with whom she had spent so many winter months.

She released her grip and stepped back, to look him up and down, hardly believing that he was really there. As she did so, a well-remembered, acid-toned voice broke in upon her enjoyment, 'Abigail Martin! What do you mean going around and engaging in displays of affection with uncouth creatures like this man. Furthermore, look at the way you're dressed! It's positively disgusting! Go and take off that awful-looking garb at once! Do you hear me?'

And Abbie turned to confront the shrewish features of Aunt Sarah looking horrified at her appearance, while behind her stood George Martin, her uncle, shaking his head at his wife's tirade and looking more than a little bemused.

Before Abbie had a chance to respond to either Billy's greeting or Aunt Sarah's admonitions, there was yet another interruption as Joey plucked at her arm and exclaimed excitedly, ' 'Scuse me, ma'am. Marty Rudd's a-comin' down the street an' he's loaded for bear. He said ter tell you it's either him or you.'

Abbie thanked the little man and stepped down off the boardwalk into the dusty rut-filled street, ignoring the shrill, querulous noise behind her of, 'Abigail Martin! Come back here. I haven't finished speaking to you!'

Coming down the street towards her, well-fortified with a few of his better quality whiskies, was the figure of the owner of the Bonanza Saloon. After he had rushed out of the city meeting, he had returned to his establishment, and had spent the day brooding over the unexpected change in his fortunes. He had always been a good gun-hand and felt confident that in a showdown he would emerge the winner.

Abbie studied him closely as he came closer. Marty packed his gun low on the right side, in a tied-down holster, the true mark of the professional gun-hand. As Billy had told her months earlier, she watched Marty's eyes, waiting for the signal that might tell her he intended to pull his pistol.

The signal came, and they both drew, but Abbie was fractionally faster as she half-turned and dropped into the crouch which had become traditional for her. Her pinfire pistol swung up as she locked her left hand around the frame forward of the trigger guard. At the same time, her left thumb was cocking the hammer, as her right index finger squeezed the trigger. Her pistol spoke twice and Marty Rudd was suddenly aware that he had made an awful mistake as he was slammed backwards, the unfired gun dropping from his hand. He hit the ground, rolled over and lay motionless.

Abbie sheathed her revolver and stood there as if turned to stone, then turned back to the group on the boardwalk.

'Sorry, Aunt Sarah! What were you saying?'

Aunt Sarah was silent, lying crumpled in a faint on the boards, her elegant attire all crumpled around her, showing her skinny legs in their white stockings. Uncle George came forward and took her hand.

'That was well done, Abbie! Knowing you, I suppose there was no other choice?'

'None whatsoever, Uncle. And sadly there is going to be far more before the day is out! But I think our first task is to revive Aunt Sarah. I believe that there should be some smelling salts in her reticule.'

She reached down and picked up the cloth bag which had fallen from her aunt's hand. Sure enough her hand closed upon a small bottle, which she extracted and held under Aunt Sarah's nostrils. The smelling salts did the trick and soon her aunt was sitting up and then rose groggily to her feet.

She looked at Abbie and then at the body still lying in the dust of the street.

'Oh Abigail! How could you! You hadn't even been introduced!' Her sense of the civil proprieties was outraged. 'You may have hurt the gentleman!'

'No, Auntie! I didn't hurt him one little bit!' she replied grimly. 'I shot him dead!'

Aunt Sarah was speechless for once in her life and stared at Abbie in horror.

'Now I think that we had better get all of you people off the street as it is very likely going to become a battleground in a very short while. When I get time I'll give you a complete explanation, but there's no time for that now. Mrs O'Brien, I suggest that you put all of your guests in a back room as the rooms facing the street may be subject to stray bullets if the guns start shooting.'

The Irish landlady nodded her head and shepherded the four people from the coach back into her own little comfortable parlour.

Uncle George returned to the boardwalk to where Abbie stood talking to Billy Curtis. Billy was telling her how he had a yearning to do some more travelling as it had become very lonely in the hidden valley once Abbie had left. He had decided to use the coach since he still had a few problems with his leg and rode as an outside passenger as it was more interesting up top rather than stuck inside.

Abbie introduced her uncle to Billy and explained how she and the old trapper had spent so many months together and how Billy had made a westerner out of a greenhorn.

'Now, Abbie, what is the situation here? You would seem to be facing the threat of an armed struggle. Is there anything I can do to help?'

Abbie smiled at her well-meaning uncle and shook her head as she very briefly outlined the issue facing the defenders and the role of Fenton, the man who had been supposedly looking after her father's interests. 'There's going to be a showdown today one way or another, but I intend to try to resolve the issues without too much shooting if I can.'

At that moment Miguel came into view riding fast but not frantically so as to avoid panicking any of the townspeople. He halted in front of Abbie and threw her a semi-military salute. '*Señorita*! Fenton and his men will be here in less than five minutes.'

Abbie turned to Jack, 'Very well, Jack! It's your show now. Make sure you have all the riflemen in position, but don't give the order to fire until I try to settle this affair peaceably.'

Jack nodded and strode down the street, stressing to his well-hidden defenders to hold their fire until ordered to shoot. He then returned to stand by Abbie, Miguel and Billy, Uncle George having at his niece's insistence retreated to the doorway of the rooming house.

There was a far-off roar, like surf bearing on a distant shore. The sound grew louder and amidst the roar could be heard individual male voices raised in anger. Then the

156

column of marching men appeared at the end of the street. They weren't as soldiers would march, in step with their arms swinging in unison, but rather they swarmed, some marching, some leaping and running, with the odd man riding astride a horse, a mule and one even on a burro. One and all, they were brandishing a weird variety of weapons ranging from sporting and military rifles, scatterguns, every type of pistol imaginable and even two or three with pitchforks. At their head rode Roger Fenton astride a handsome black mare and flanked by two of his gun-hands.

The marchers advanced until they were no more than twelve to fifteen feet away from the waiting trio when Abbie cried out in a loud voice, 'Halt!' Without pausing she went on quickly, 'Don't do anything foolish. We have no desire to see bloodshed. Now is the time for some honest talking!'

Fenton looked at the three people blocking his path and called out, 'Don't pay any attention to these three. They're just bluffing!'

He raised his arm as a signal for his followers to press forward and Jack put a small silver whistle to his lips and blew a long blast.

Immediately riflemen came into view on rooftops and windows, behind barricades and in the wagons blocking the side streets. There was the audible sound of hammers being cocked and the miners in the centre of the street looked at each other in dismay.

Abbie stepped forward, 'Neighbours! If I may call you that. Please place your guns on the ground and listen to me. Nobody intends to do you any harm. However, we will defend ourselves. I do not know what Roger Fenton has told you, but what I'm going to tell you is the truth and I am quite willing to show the evidence I possess to prove my case.'

She went on to state who she was, told them about her father's will, his properties and investments and how she and friends had discovered how the man who was leading them was a liar, cheat, thief and a murderer.

The miners listened carefully under the guns of the Colorado City defenders. Initially they received Abbie's story with scepticism, but as her details became known a low growl of anger directed at their former employer filled the air. Frantically Fenton looked at the two men riding either side of him.

'What do you think I've been paying you for! Do something!'

'We sure will, Fenton!'

Both men raised their hands high above their heads and, looking down at Abbie, said, 'Ma'am, we just resigned from this man's employment. Is it OK if we leave the territory?'

Abbie nodded, and with hands still held high they rode off leaving Fenton white-faced at the way his hold on the community had just trickled away from him.

The miners moved towards him and their intention was clear when some of them started uttering cries of, 'Get a rope!' and 'String 'im up!'

Fenton suddenly dropped from his saddle and turned towards Abbie, 'You meddlin' bitch! This is all of your doing! But you aren't going to live to enjoy it!'

So saying, he grabbed for his holstered pistol. His movements were clumsy, indicating he had always preferred to have others do his shooting for him, but Abbie wasn't prepared to be merciful. She waited until his Colt had cleared its holster, before drawing and shooting in one fluid movement. Her aim was true, and Roger Fenton was thrown back by her bullet, and fell beneath his horse's hoofs where he lay motionless.

There's not too much more to tell at this time. Abbie had Jack open the Bonanza to allow the thirsty miners to have a couple of free beers each before they headed back to their quarters with her promise to be out to negotiate a fresh working agreement with them as soon as possible.

Bobby Smith was asked if he thought that he could manage the Bonanza saloon, under the eagle eye of his mother of course. The young man was puffed up with pride at the responsibility and declared that, 'As sure as tootin' I'll do a great job.'

Abbie's next step was to lower significantly all the rents on the various properties still held in trust accounts in her father's name, with the understanding that the people renting could purchase said properties at any time.

Jack was appointed financial manager and it was agreed that he and Dora would live at and supervise the horse ranch, which eventually Abbie intended to use as her headquarters.

Miguel Garcia and his two fellow Mexicans were now eager to return to their families, seeing that all Abbie's problems appeared to be solved. They were sent off back to William Bent with a pack horse loaded with all sorts of supplies and each man was the happy possessor of five gold double eagles.

Abbie tried hard to persuade Billy Curtis to settle down in the area but the old trapper was adamant, 'Abbie! I'd just be gettin' itchy feet from time to time. I can't see myself being tied to one place forever. I'll be droppin' by ter see you now and then. An' you know you'd always be welcome in my hidden valley.'

And early one morning he was gone without a word to anyone. That was Billy's way.

Aunt Sarah's and Uncle George's quest to discover the fate of the missing Penravens was accomplished. They stayed several weeks and, as Abbie's relatives, were made welcome everywhere they went in and around Colorado City before finally heading back east and returning to England, much to Aunt Sarah's relief. Several times she tried to pressure Abbie into going back with them, but it was of no use. Abbie's heart was in the raw, untamed west. Finally, one day Sarah played what she thought was her trump card, 'But, Abbie, if you stay here you may have money, but that's all. In England you have a title.'

'Dear Aunt Sarah, you are so wrong! Here I do have a title, which means a lot to me. I'm the Pinfire Lady!'